A Lancer's Tale

Leon Michaels

Books by Leon Michaels
Stand Alone Action/Adventure

The Path Home

From the Mists of Darkness

Task Force Nemesis

Tales From The Bench

The Echelon Factor

Yesterday is Today's Tomorrow

Stand Alone ScFi

The Morbius Expedition

Random Acts Of Science Fiction

Yesterday is Today's Tomorrow

Willem

A Lancer's Tale

Post- Apocalyptic

Three Against The Darkness

"The Crane Equation Trilogy"

The Crane Equation: The Early Years

The Crane Equation: Rebuilding a Nation

The Crane Equation: The Crane Legacy

Action/Adventure

"The Black Ops Series"

Operation Damocles

Operation Dokkaebi

Operation Yofune-Nushi

Operation Kartikeya

The Black Orchid

The Twenty-First Special Operations Group: Book One: Family

The Twenty-First Special Operations Group: Book Two: Operators

Operation Heracles

Operation Pandora

ScFi-Action/Adventure

"The Denoyelles Family Saga"

The Hanover Throne

The Bellus Project

The Bellus Legacy

The Bellus Myth

The Bellus Solution

The Bellus Prophecy

The Phoenix Project

The Bellus Curse

Acknowledgements

As Always, to my Wife and chief Editor, for the time spent reading my gibberish, for the evil use of an Red Pen, and for telling me that a specific sentence or twelve makes absolutely no sense at all.

Thank You Dear!!!

To Emersen. She knows why.

This is a work of Fiction. Any similarities to individuals past or present is unintentional and purely a coincidence. Any similarities to any individual in the future is pure Karma.

This Page Left Intentionally Blank

Prologue

The Federation Free Lance Infantry was formed on the planet Aurora by Colonel Wagner Dubois, a former member of the Federation Fleet Marines after his retirement. As with many men and women who had spent most of the adult life in uniform, he was at a loss in how to spend the rest of his life.

He gathered trusted men and women he had known in service and established a single company of mercenaries to be known as the Federation Free Lance Infantry. He set the standards high for his Lancers unlike most mercenary units roaming the Federation, taking contracts where they could find them.

Within a decade the First Lancer Regiment was formed growing from the original company. Over the decades and long after Colonel Dubois's death, the Lancers as they became known as grew into three regiments and were used by the Federation to put down rebellions within the Federation, always on the side of the elected Governments of the planets involved.

When disinherited Conrad Denoyelles was asked to return to Hanover, to take the Hanover Throne over the three worlds of the Hanover System, he was a Lancer Captain, and in returning to Hanover, he quietly brought his old Regiment with him to support his move to change the system from a feudal system to a democratic one.

As the Count Denoyelles, he fought the corruption within his own world's system then exposed the corruption that had infested the original Federation Council and Congress. Count Conrad had monetary resources far greater than most planetary systems at his command and when it appeared that the Federation was threatening violence to bring the Hanover system back under their control, the entire Lancer Command moved from Aurora to Hanover and established their headquarters and bases there.

The Lancers had one basic rule. Service in the Fleet Navy or Marines before applying. The only exceptions were the Centaurians who, both sexes, were taught the skills of close combat from the crib, especially with razor sharp blades. And there was another exception for those who could pass the muster after eight weeks of grueling training that even the former service members were required to pass. It seemed a contradiction to the basic rule, but the initial testing removed many who thought they had what it took to pass muster, where the old hands understood the game and were able to move past it and onto further training.

It had long been noted that many of the men and women who joined the Lancers suffered the memories and nightmares of their previous careers. They entered under their own names or if the chose, under a new name to conceal their past. In many ways the Lancers were a modern version of the old French Foreign Legion of Earth.

Walking Through Hell

Eli was tense as he walked through the smoldering ruins of the village the Rebels had decided to hold, instead of retreating as they had been for the past week. The darkness hid secrets while the flickering flames reflected off his gold tinted face shield, and his filters barely held off the scent of burnt or burning bodies. Behind him lay his team medic with half his head blown off as he was treating Spencer, his Assistant Team Leader, who was missing most of his right leg. Spencer would survive his wound, but that gave little comfort to Eli as he walked point with the remaining three members of his team.

Even with his helmet's AI filtering out a lot of the background noise and dampening the flickering light from flames, Eli could feel sensory overload creeping up on him. In a battlefield such as this, you had to look at everything, regardless how innocent it may look to the casual observer. On the ground in front of him was part of an arm, with the hand still tightly wrapped around the grip of a carbine. Eli stepped over the object and continued moving forward. Months before a man in another battalion had kicked such an object out of his path without realizing the hand held a primed grenade. The grenade dislodged from the hand, exploding seconds later crippling him and killing the man behind him. Some lessons are harsher than others.

Corporal Eli Gambit was the Alpha Team Leader for Second Section, Fox Company, Second Battalion, Seventh Lancer Regiment, and this was not his first dance. The proper name for the Lancers was The Federation Freelance Infantry, but over the centuries the organization was just known as The Lancers. And to be a Lancer, whether you were male or female, you were a mercenary. But Eli Gambit did not start out his military life as a mercenary, the same as nearly every member of the Lancers.

There was no doubt in Eli's mind he was scared, and he doubted he could find a Lancer anywhere who would claim they were not scared during a drop, or movement to contact. Anyone who claimed they were never scared you avoided with a passion. The legend of the courage of the Lancers was just a myth based upon the fact they threw everything they could into a fight, and never gave a meter of ground to whomever they were fighting. And here in the darkness of this ruined village gave truth to what the Lancers could do to those that stood before them to fight. The mortars of Fox Company had laid ruin to the village once the fighting had started, but that did not help Eli's medic or Assistant Team Leader.

His earpiece crackled.

"Eli, hold what you've got. First section is coming up to relieve you."

Eli dropped to one knee and continued to search in front of him for anything that might harm him.

"Roger, holding in place. Eli Out."

Everyone had call signs, but under the stress of combat, most ignored them and just used the individual's name, unless there was a conflict of having two or more people with the same name. Often at that point their last names were used, but he was the only Eli Gambit in the Lancers, and like most Lancers, Gambit was not his real name.

The lead element of the First Section had not even made it to his position when he received a call from the only female on his team.

"Eli, this is Cher, you need to see what I have found, over."

Eli looked right, then left as his AI indicated where his people had spread out as they waited for the First section. He moved to his left thirty meters to join up with Cher. She pointed down at a body nearly lying in front of her. Eli had his AI enhance his vision and what he saw was not to his liking. He told his AI to go to the Company Net.

"Fox, this is Eli, be advised we have a stiff here wearing the uniform and insignia of the Denali Rangers. I say again, we may have Denali Rangers to our front. Out"

10

Like the Lancers, the Denali Rangers were mercenaries, but with the reputation of ignoring the rules of combat, and even booby-trapping infants in order to kill or slow down anyone in pursuit of them on the battle field. They were even known to booby-trap their own wounded and dead.

The Federation had tried for years to remove the Rangers, but they were slippery, moving from one planet to another, hiding out in the open, and only took contacts they felt they would complete before the Federation arrived to clean up their mess.

Cher, also known as Specialist Cherry Blossom was a red headed Centaurian and she was the team explosives expert. Her name was a joke, a play on her flaming red fur, and very few people knew her real name, Clare Bennington.

She reached into her leg pouch and removed a packet from it. Inside was thirty meters of ultra-strong line made of micro twist fibers with a folding treble hook. She carefully opened the hook, locking its prongs in place, then she leaned over and hooked it into the opposite side of the body in front of her.

Cher nodded to Eli who began backing away from the body as she moved a different direction from him. Eli came back up on the company net.

"Fox, this is Eli, Cherry is hooked onto the Ranger and is about to roll the body over. Fire in the hole!"

When Cherry felt she was far enough away and had gone prone, she looked around to see that Eli had also laid down. He was the only person she was concerned with at the moment and once she was comfortable with the situation, she also called out on the company net.

"This is Cher...... fire in the hole!"

With that she pulled hard on the line moving the body until is was now lying flat on its back. Cher watched the chronometer in the lower right of her helmet's display for three minutes to insure a delayed charge was not in play. Once the clock had ran the time, she got up on her hands and knees and began moving to the body.

11

Eli watched from his position and just laid still, watching Cher move to the body. Cher was not taking any chances by standing up at this point in the game, and with the First section having already taken the point, Eli was not concerned about someone shooting at them as Cher went to check the body for other explosive devices, then intelligence.

Fox Company slowly moved past Eli and his team as Cher carefully examined the body in case there were other hidden devices on it. Even rolling the body over could have activated a device that just needed a bit more jostling to set it off.

"Cher, this is Fox One, how is it going, over?"

"Fox One, how many times do I have to tell you to leave me the hell alone when I'm working, over!"

There was quiet from the other end of that conversation, but Eli could swear he heard light laughter from the tail end of Fox Company which had just passed him. He looked at his helmet chronometer to see that sunrise was roughly an hour away and lying as he was, he found he was fighting sleep. It had been a long night of movement and fighting.

"Eli, come take a look at this."

Cher's call shook him out of his stupor. He carefully moved to her knowing the body and area was clean, otherwise she would not have called for him. When he got close enough, she handed him a hard copy photograph. He looked at it then handed it back to her.

"Fox One this is Eli, we need Intel to collect the Ranger's body and documents, over."

"Eli, already contacted them, Fox One out."

Eli raised his face shield and looked at Cher as she raised hers.

"Cher, keep that to yourself, understand."

She looked at him for a moment, then leaned close and kissed him.

"Yeah, mums the word, but I bet its going to mess up any plans I had once we boost off this shithole."

"Well, such is the life of a Lancer. Make sure that Intel fills out the proper paperwork when you transfer the body and documents over to them. Chain of custody is important in this matter, understand?"

"No problem Eli."

Eli moved back to his former position before she could steal another kiss from him. He knew having her for a lover, even a part time lover was not the best of plans considering their positions in the section, although she would never play that off against him, but loosing her in a fight would not be something he wanted to consider.

Epsilon Company moved through behind Fox and just before daylight passed through Fox's lines, then ran head onto the dug-in Rebels. But the Rebels had lost a lot of men and equipment in the village and Epsilon quickly overran their positions.

As Epsilon was engaged, Battalion Intelligence arrived to take the body and documents in hand along with a video statement from Cher concerning how she found the body and the documents she took off it. They asked Eli if he had seen the documents, and he only told them he had seen the one photo and that was all. Eli and Cher were told to return to the drop zone with the body while the remaining members of his team were to merry up with the Fox Company Command section during the rest of the operation.

They boarded an Armored Assault boat with the body and the Captain from the Intel Section, then lifted to their troop carrier in orbit. They were isolated from each other once aboard the carrier.

Questions

Eli sat in the ship's conference room with his gear stacked on the table, cleaning his carbine and sipping on a cup of coffee. He was wishing he could take a shower and put on a clean uniform, but he had not been given the chance upon boarding the transport.

At the far end of the room was the Battalion's Intel Captain in conversation with the ship's Intel Officer as they were going through the items from the dead Ranger's body. He had no idea where Cher was, but figured her situation was no better than his own.

A Med-Tech entered the conference room, handed a file over to the Intel officers and left without saying a word to him. It was probably the primarily autopsy report on the dead Ranger. The report was passed between the officers before they moved to where Eli was reassembling his carbine.

It was the Lancer Captain that opened the discussion.

"Corporal Gambit, do you have any idea why that Ranger had a photo of you?"

"No Captain, and I have no idea who he was either. I did not recognize him."

"We have a theory that it was in case they laid hands on prisoners, they could use you against us."

"How do you figure that Captain. I'm just a Lancer Corporal. No one of importance."

"Do you deny that was you in that photo?" This came from the Senior Lieutenant who was the ship's Intel officer.

"No Lieutenant, that was me alright, but that was a different life, and a long time ago. I don't see why anyone would think I'm important."

Both officers looked at each other before the ship's officer spoke again.

"Commander….."

Eli raised his hand to cut him off.

"Do not go there Lieutenant."

The Lieutenant started to speak, but was stopped by the Captain touching his arm.

"Eli, I think the Lieutenant was only trying to determine if this had something to do with your past."

Eli stood, picked up his vest and carbine.

"Captain, I've told you everything I know. My past is dead and buried as far as I am concerned, and let's keep it that way. I think I'm done here, so unless you gentlemen have further need of me, I'm going to my quarters, take a long hot shower, then maybe grab some sack time."

"Alright Eli. If we have something later, we'll page you."

"Thanks Captain. Lieutenant."

As soon as Eli left the room the Fleet Lieutenant returned to the subject Eli had so abruptly cut off.

"Captain, there is more to this than I believe he is telling us about that photo."

"Maybe so Lieutenant, but he is a Lancer now, with a new name and no past except for the record he makes here. The only way you can make him speak of his past is to set him before a Command Board of Inquiry, and even then you had better have your ships all in line."

"I checked the records. Commander Elijah Decker was killed during the test flight of a Minotaur Class Scout Ship. But we both know that was him sitting in that chair, and he even admitted that was a photo of him. What gives?"

"Lieutenant, I'm not going to ask and you certainly are not either. If the man says he has no idea why that photo was in that Ranger's pocket, and he had never seen that man before, then I think we should be looking elsewhere instead of wasting time on this line of thinking, don't you?"

Eli stood under the shower letting the hot water wash away five days of sweat and dirt as he was also wondering why that Ranger had that photo of him. This was one thing he liked about the Cassandra Class Transports was the availability of hot water. He might have to share quarters with three other Corporals, but there was always plenty of hot water to wash away the tension in the body.

When he had entered his quarters, he saw that Admin had already packed up Spencer's personal things for shipping to whatever hospital where they would fit him with a new, bio-mechanical leg. But the bags on Janowski's bunk caught him by surprise. Janowski was in the Company Headquarters Section which told Eli that the fighting during the night was worse than he imagined. But the bags could not tell him if Janowski was dead or badly wounded.

He laid down but could not shut his mind off from what had happened on the planet. It wasn't the fighting, or the loss of team members, it was that someone was specifically looking for him and he had no idea why.

Eli finally got back up, put on a field uniform and went to the ship's mess to get something to eat since the Lancer's Mess was closed since the Battalion was in the dirt.

He smelled her before he saw her as Cher or Cherry, always wore a Cherry fragrance cologne when not in the dirt. Eli did not turn around as he was going to let her make the move today.

"Eli, are you alive?"

"No Cherry, I'm just a ghost residing within your twisted mind."

She leaned over and kissed him on his cheek, then moved around the table, sitting her tray down then took the chair opposite him.

"Eli, what is going on? I sat in the Master of Arms office for several hours before they told me I could go to quarters. No questions or anything about that Ranger."

"It's not the Ranger they want to know about, it's the photo he had on him. Why he had it on him. Cher, leave it at that and forget you ever saw that photo."

"Good God Eli, I know who you really are. Every member of the Battalion knows who you really are. But we allow you to live the life you have chosen as a Lancer, and you are a damn fine leader. At the risk of ruining the relationship we have, is what that photo represents the reason you are in the Lancers or is there something else. Something you do not have to tell me."

"Both Cher and that is as good as you are going to receive. And no, our relationship is as it was although it should not be this way. If I get dusted, how are you going to deal with that? If it happens to you, how will I feel about it? Even if we have a dozen other lovers in our life, none of them are as close as we are when it drops in the pot."

"Eli, I've thought about that every time we fall asleep in each other's arms, and every time we drop. We're both professionals and will have to deal with what happens, if it happens."

"Yeah, I know."

He finished his meal and just sat, sipping on his cup of cooled tea as she ate. She just started on the small piece of fruit cake when she spoke to him.

"Eli, I know you're being polite, but I think you should go to your quarters and get some rest. I don't think sharing a Rec Room with you right now would be smart."

"I think you're right Cher. I was just going off what you said down in the dirt is all."

"Well, that was then, this is now. Get out of here before we make fools of ourselves."

Eli left the mess and just wandered around the ship for a bit before going to his quarters. Because of the shared rooms, the ship had special rooms within the Recreational deck for couples to use so they would not be disturbed by roommates. No one commented about who was using them with whom, and it was just a fact of life that mixed units, males and females, were going to engage in sexual activity and as long as it did not interfere with the function of the units, no one paid any attention to the activity.

He finally fell asleep and in doing so, past memories returned that he wished were buried.

Planet QX-3397

Eli sat at the controls of his Tempest Class Scout Ship watching as the Fleet's Hornet Fighters were mixing it up with the alien craft swarming around the planet only known as QX-3397. He was a full Commander in command of six Scout Ships deep inside unknown space off the Eastern Rim of Federation space.

The on again and off again war with these aliens had been going on for decades with the aliens loosing hundreds of their mining craft against the fire power of the Fleet's ships. It wasn't until the Tempest Class Scout Ship that those specific vessels had any chance of survival against the over-powered plasma bolts of the aliens.

When alien activity along the rim was detected, Eli and his Scouts were sent in to determine their status. There were hundreds of alien mining craft ripping apart QX-3397 which was a dead, airless planet. The small mining craft had grapplers to take hold of large rocks, or enemy craft and a plasma cannon unlike anything the Federation had, producing an extremely powerful burst of plasma which they used to break up the planet, or as a weapon against other ships.

As Eli was pulling his Scouts back from the aliens, to just leave them alone, the aliens sortied from the planet against his Scouts. Each Scout launched a volley of six Excalibur missiles against the aliens as they pulled back with the Fleet's Hornet Fighters moving forward to tangle with the aliens.

Sensor data showed all thirty-six missiles found targets as Eli positioned the Scouts in a picket line to observe the fight in front of them and if necessary, to recovered any pilot that had to eject his cockpit due to battle damage.

The twenty-two Hornets were tangling with over two hundred of the alien crafts and eliminating them as fast as they could acquire a lock on the vessels. One of the Hornets finally took a hard hit and the cockpit was ejected with it's small booster engines pushing it back towards the picket line.

Eli watched as the aliens went after the cockpit with two Hornets doing their best to protect their fellow pilot. He kicked his ships engines into boost and went to try to retrieve the cockpit. Eli launched a full spread of missiles at the gathering aliens knowing the missiles would ignore the Hornets and the cockpit.

As Eli gained on the cockpit, he knew that he would not be able to retrieve it and fight off the aliens at the same time. He moved between the cockpit and the aliens and fired off another volley of missiles as his co-pilot was sweeping up targets with the turret mounted plasma cannon on top of the Scout ship. He got a green light on his missile tubes and fired another salvo.

His head's up display showed that the last of his missiles were in the tubes and ready for launch. His two gunners had extended the side mounted plasma cannons and were working them against the approaching aliens as the ship began taking hits from the aliens plasma bolts. He fired off the last of his missiles and watched as they found targets.

"Gambler One this is Three, we have the pod, get out of there!"

Eli looked at his situation board and knew he could not just turn tail and expose the weakest part of his ship to the aliens, but his shields and Dimex armor was taking a beating. Just as he was ready to make his move away from the fight, he was hit by four separate plasma bursts against his port cannon mount and the last burst of plasma entered the ship, killing his two gunners and sending his ship spinning back towards the picket line.

As he fought to gain control of the ship, he was hit again and he could feel the heat of this burst against his battle suit. He heard screaming and looked over at his co-pilot to see his left arm gone at the shoulder, The screaming was short lived as Pennebrook died in his seat.

Eli looked at the turret control panel to see it was still in the green and put it in automatic mode. As long as the cannon had power and a sensor feed, it would continue fighting as he fought to save his ship.

20

He looked out his observation window to see Hornets eating away at his attackers and the bolts of his own cannon removing threats until another bolt rocked the ship and the cannon control panel went red. Eli applied boost but the panel turned red, telling him he was now stuck in whatever condition he was in. He just sat back and closed his eyes as he felt another burst hit his ship then another hit underneath the ship and he blacked out from the effect it had on his body.

Eli woke to the bright lights of the whatever room he was in, feeling as if every bone in his body was broken, and every nerve alight to the sensation of being burned. But he was in no pain and wondered if he was actually dead.

It would take a year before he could walk without crutches or a cane. He stood in full uniform and was awarded the Fleet's Medal of Valor with Starburst Cluster for his actions during the battle of Planet QX-3397 in protecting the Hornet pilot from being killed after his fighter had been destroyed.

Sensor data showed all twenty-four of his Excalibur missiles had confirmed kills and his cannons accounted for seventeen more alien ships before his own ship was completely disabled.

Eli could not understand receiving the medal for loosing his ship and getting his three men killed to save the life of one man. Granted, this was the job he volunteered for, but to receive an award only made the loss of his men worse.

He petitioned the Admiral of the Federation Fleet to arrange for him to disappear once his time was up since the publicity concerning his actions were known across the Federation. The Minotaur Project was already scrapped and they used it to declare him dead after a much publicized transfer into the program.

Eli wandered for nearly two years before he walked into a Federation Embassy on LaGrange and spoke to the Lancer Senior Lieutenant in charge of the Embassy's security. He enlisted as a Private and was sent to Keres to join the Regiment there and to begin training.

Aftermath

Eli woke covered in sweat and the knowledge he had relived that battle once again. He went into the refresher, turned the shower on cold and just stood under the water, letting it flow into his mouth the help rinse the sour taste from his mouth.

After the shower he checked his chronometer to see he had been asleep for over six hours. He knew what he had to do now, but there were loose ends he needed to tie off before he took the step. He went to the Rec Center first to see if Cher was around but no one had seen her in the area. Then to the Mess without luck. Next stop was too her quarters but she had to be out and about, otherwise she would have answered the door buzzer.

He found her in the canteen talking to one of the ship's Lancers and the look on her face was she was about ready to strike. Eli walked up to her and just laid his hand on her shoulder. She looked up at him then back to the Lancer and apologized to him because she had another date she had forgotten all about.

In the Rec Room once the door was closed her attitude changed.

"Alright Eli, what was that all about?"

"What do you mean Cher?"

"You've seen me hook up with other men before, hell you have even seen me enter these rooms with another man before and you have never said or did a thing to prevent it. Why tonight?"

"Because I'm leaving Clare."

Using her real name set her back some.

"Leaving? Are they transferring you?"

"No Clare, I'm cashing out before I get you or others killed because of who I am?"

"So you decided to have one last screw before you leave?"

22

"Clare, I've never just screwed you and you know it. I just wanted to spend some time with you before I walk away."

She sat down on one of the small chairs in the room and just looked at Eli.

"No, even the first time it felt as you were making love to me, not just screwing me for the enjoyment. What are you going to do?"

"I've got money so I can pretty much do whatever I want. Maybe go out to one of the new worlds, get a piece of ground and take up farming. As crazy as it sounds, I do know a bit about farming."

"Then let me go with you. You'll need someone to watch your back for you."

"Clare, then I'd be putting you right back in the situation I am trying to avoid. At least here you'd be armed to the teeth and have others watching your back. No Clare, as tempting as it is, I can't risk it."

She looked at her chronometer.

"Word is we have about fourteen hours before the Battalion lifts. Think we can find something to do during that time?"

"We'll think of something doll."

She stood and began removing her clothes as he also started removing his. They met beside the bed and there was no doubt in his mind that tonight was going to get wild as she was even more aggressive than the first time they joined in a Rec Room.

When the Battalion lifted, Eli felt as if he had ran a marathon and Cher/Clare walked as if she had a rash, but with a smile on her face.

Eli did not have to arrange a meeting with the Battalion Commander as he was called for as the troops were offloading from their assault boats. The Battalion Sergeant Major escorted him to the Transport Captain's stateroom where he found himself in the company of the Battalion's senior officers along with the ship's senior staff. The Battalion Commander opened the discussion.

"Corporal Gambit, please, take a seat."

"Colonel, are you sitting a Board of Inquiry?"

"No Corporal, although it has been suggested, but we both know it would be a waste of time, don't we?"

"Yes Sir, so may I now ask what is going on here?"

"Sit, we have some information that you need to hear."

Eli sat on a chair as the rest got comfortable where they could in the state room and waited for someone to speak. It was the Battalion Intelligence Officer that broke the silence.

"Corporal Gambit, besides the results of the DNA search on the Ranger brought up with you, we captured two Rangers during the clean-up after you lifted. The DNA search came back belonging to a David Atherton, former Fleet Marine, discharged as undesirable for service. Is that name familiar to you?"

"Yes Major, it is."

"Care to expound on that statement?"

"No Sir because if you have his name, you have his records and those will tell you everything you need to know about him and any relationship he may have to me. But as my official statement concerning him still stands as I have never met or seen him before in my life, Sir."

"But his name is familiar to you?"

Eli sighed.

"Yes Sir, his brother often spoke of him."

"Corporal Gambit, according to the prisoners we took, he was out looking for you. Hoping to kill you himself in revenge for his brother's death."

"If that is the case Major, then someone had best inform Fleet Headquarters there has been a breech in security. The individual who took Samuel Atherton into combat is dead according to the official record. If they do not have a breech in security, then the Lancers most certainly has one."

Eli just sat and looked at the Intelligence Major without expression.

"Eli, what are you going to do about this situation? If he was after you, is it possible other members of the family will try to find you, to kill you?" The Battalion Commander asked.

"Colonel, I was going to ask for an appointment with you so I could cash out of the Lancers. I cannot risk getting a Lancer killed because someone was specifically targeting me. It's one thing to lose people in battle, but not like that. I cannot and will not live with such on my conscious."

"Corporal Gambit, I will grant your exit from the Lancers because of your concern for the safety of those you serve with. Captain Smythe, please process him out immediately. Now there are four Scout ships standing by for orders, we'll arrange for one to take you where ever you wish as soon as the paperwork is complete. Go gather you things."

The Colonel and others stood as Eli stood with the Colonel stepping forward to offer his hand.

"May the Saints watch over you Eli."

"Thank you Colonel."

Eli returned to his quarters and packed. His remaining roommates were still getting their gear and men squared away and had not returned to the room. Once packed, he went to the Battalion Admin office and signed his discharge, then cashed out his Lancer account in cash.

When he started to leave the Admin Office for the docking port where the Scout ship was waiting, the Battalion Sergeant Major met him in the corridor with a non-descript bag in his hand.

"Corporal you left a bag in your room that I do believe you may have need of in the future."

Eli looked at the bag thinking what it contained was his weapons and body armorer with battle vest and helmet.

"Are you positive that is my bag Sergeant Major?"

"According to the Colonel it is, and who are we to argue with the Colonel?"

"Tell the Colonel I said thanks."

When Eli arrived at the docking port, he saw Cher standing at the end of the corridor. He started to go to her but she shook her head no, then smiled and blew him a kiss before walking from view into a connecting corridor.

All the Scout ship pilot asked was where to take him.

"What's the newest world in this sector?"

"Gander."

"Then take me there and put me down away from any settlements."

"Yes Sir."

A New Name

Eli was set down five kilometers outside the Smithville settlement on Gander just before dawn. He made his way to the settlement, specifically to the crude space port and made inquiries of the two freighter's at the port. After arranging transport on one of them, he went into the settlement and sold most of his old uniforms to a resale shop while purchasing clothing more suited to his new identity and plan.

When Eli left the Fleet, he left with two sets of identification to use as he made his way through life. He burned the first set when he joined the Lancers and now he opened the new set which had been sealed in his gear until needed.

His new identity was that of Ezra Connors from Hastings.

He knew that the identification would withstand the most critical scrutiny as it had been constructed by the Federation Intelligence Agency along with the Federation Auditing Office. Ezra Connors was at one time a real person, but had died at the age of eleven during a raid by slavers on their planet. Records now showed he survived as an orphan, educated at a minor, two year university, then joined the Fleet as a Gunner's Mate.

It was not that he was anyone special in the universe, or related to anyone of importance. He had not done anything different than dozens of pilots had done during their careers, but that specific moment in time changed his life forever, and with the change came a debt to him he felt was uncalled for, but took advantage of it as he felt he could never lead men as he once did.

This was also where his life didn't make sense as he joined the Lancers in search for something of value in his life. The nightmares of that battle only returned when he became too stressed, but never affected him in combat as a Lancer. It was as if he found a calm place in the chaos of battle.

But now he felt he had to run from the possibility that if one member of the Atherton family might come looking for him, others might follow suit, especially if it is found that David

Atherton was killed in a battle where he had led Lancers into that village.

Within the Ezra Connors identity was a Fleet Pension paid quarterly to an account that had set for years, drawing the pension and paying interest against the money as he served in the Lancers under a different name. This on top of a one time payment for services rendered through a commercial account linked to the Throne.

Ezra Connors spent two years traveling from planet to planet either paying for the transit or working as a deck hand on the old freighters to pay his way. Along the way he transferred his battle gear and weapons to a secure transport case to keep them hidden from prying eyes, along with other things he picked up along the way.

Three sectors from where he had left the Lancers, near the Northern Rim, Ezra found himself on a frontier planet by the name of Nemea. At the Federation's Settlement Office in Eurydice on Nemea, he carefully examined the holo-maps of the planet at the unclaimed land available to him, and the soil reports, then selected a large partial, over four thousand hectares in a valley including the surrounding hills and paid the settler's fees sight unseen.

During the time in transit during the past two years, Ezra as he now thought of himself, had physical contact with only one female during a transit between worlds as a passenger with another passenger during the two week flight. He stayed in Eurydice for a week gathering the things he needed to start a new life and was able to deflect the advances of a waitress in the café at the small hotel he was staying at.

He figured if he was just passing through, the waitress would have been a nice disruption in his sexual drought, but making this world a home meant avoiding such contact until he felt the time was right. It could cause too many disruptions in his life.

Ezra had upgraded his computer pad during a layover on Zyra before moving on and he often accessed the public information site for the Lancers. He was sitting in the café eating breakfast when he came across a notification tagged to the Seventh Lancer Regiment of Cher getting married to the Lancer Liaison Officer to Princess Consuela. They had met when she was posted to the Palace as part of the Princess's security detachment. He just smiled thinking how lucky that Major was having her all to himself.

The valley he claimed was one hundred and twenty kilometers from Eurydice and he bought a used, but in good condition fusion generator driven six wheel drive, all terrain truck capable of hauling four metric tons in its bed.

When he left Eurydice, he had a train behind him made up of a six ton trailer loaded with farming equipment for the tractor that was behind it. He had already arranged for a contractor to come into the valley a week later to build his home once he determined exactly where he wanted it built.

Because of the load he was carrying and pulling, plus the lack of any manner of improved roads, it took Ezra three days to enter his valley. He selected a building site next to a small river cutting through the valley after carefully inspecting the terrain for how far the river might overflow during the wet season.

He staked out the location of the house and out buildings then just waited for the contractor to arrive with the materials he would need to build the house based upon the prints he had confirmed, and left with the contractor.

A New Life

He was born on Earth and raised in the mass farming region of the Mid-West on the North American continent. His father was a Horticulture Specialists and his mother was a Botanist. They worked for one of the largest farming enterprises on Earth and Ezra had learned from the crib how to farm the land.

Ezra spent his youth working the soil as his parent's hoped he would follow them in their work. It was in the university that his desire to leave Earth was developed when he met a Centaurian female named Gwyneth, that turned him inside out, both in and out of bed.

Gwyneth was taking courses in Horticulture so she could take the lessons learned there back to her home world of Zyra, but the courses he took in Astronomy gave him the itch to see the stars, and once he had graduated, he joined the Fleet. He was selected for Officer's Training while in Fleet Basic and from there he trained in Scout Ships.

Promotions came fast for Ezra as his skills with the ships and his manner of handling his crews were noted. It was noted he was patient in his dealings and had a high mechanical aptitude which helped in the small, self-contained Scout ships.

He stood looking at the chest high grass of the valley thinking there was profit in that grass if the Bio-mass readings were within the guides for feeding cattle. Ezra cut four stalks of the tall grass and put them through the Biological Analyzer he had bought to help insure quality of any crops he grew. This was something he had learned from his mother before he was ten years old. The tests came back with a high positive and he knew then how to start his farming.

Ezra checked his accounts via the Uni-web and noted he had already spent nearly forty percent of his total funds at that point. He still had plenty to live on plus the pension he received from the Fleet would help cover any short comings over the next few years, but he had to make this a paying proposition otherwise he was wasting his time. He ordered the cutters, rakes and balers to produce hay, then went to work laying out the fields as the contractor was building his house and barns.

Soon he was cutting the tall grass to allow it to dry before raking then baling. He did his daily maintenance checks on his tractor and attachments to insure he could complete his clearing of the ground so he could then turn around and plow it. When he realized the speed in which the grass was growing behind him, he had to change his plans and began plowing the mowed fields, then back to cutting and baling again.

He published a notice on the planet's buy/sell net of the hay but he got lucky when an off world buyer saw his ad and contacted him about supplying the hay to another planet that was suffering a drought and needed the hay for the ranches.

Ezra sold the hay at the going rate on Nemea with the added note in the contract that the buyer was responsible for moving the large, round bales from his farm to the space port at Eurydice for shipment off planet.

He stopped plowing and just focused on the hay crop at this time, allowing the plowed earth to grow back the grass. But as profitable it was, the hours were beginning to wear on him. He put an ad in the planet's net for farm workers and soon had to build a bunk house for three young men he hired to help him.

The first two shipments off world also paid for two more tractors to deal with the work load, and by the time the fourth shipment was lifted, he was showing a nice profit after payroll, materials, along with room and board for his hired help.

Ezra sat in his home office looking over the books for the first year and wondered where time had gone. There was no doubt in his mind that he was as lucky as lucky could get, and from the contracts on his desk to buy his hay, he was wondering when the bottom would fall out of the market.

The drought on Paschal could not last forever and others were starting to bale hay seeing his success. He now had six hands working for him and they hustled six days a week for him with him declaring the calendar Sunday as a day of rest.

Part of his luck was he had settled early in the planetary spring and although the fall and winter had slowed the grass, the winters in this region were always mild according to the planetary records. And even though the winters were wet, they were never to the point the work had to completely stop for weeks or months to bring in the next crop of hay.

When the property was finally surveyed in, he owned forty-three hundred hectares of ground with twenty-one hundred in grass with the rest in old growth timber. Although there was plenty of hardwoods in the timber, there were no exotics, but lumber is lumber. Ezra began making plans to harvest and mill his own lumber for his own use and sales.

But with success also came problems. The one problem that was on his mind as he looked over the books was that he had to report to the Settler's Office with his books to show his claim was viable and that he was being successful in his endeavors. Ezra thought it was ridicules that he had to prove his claim was successful, when it was widely known he was shipping tons of hay out monthly.

A part of the problem with going into Eurydice was not that he would be on the farm to insure the work was getting done because the hands had learned early on they would benefit from their labors with bonuses if he did not have to look over their shoulders every day. He had laid out what needed to be done the five days he expected to be gone and was certain those tasks would be complete when he returned.

But within that problem was the sister to one of his hands by the name of Susanne Wetherspoon. She was twenty-six, stood about one point eight meters and worked in the Settler's Office. She had came to take her brother, Simon home for the Saint's Holiday and made it obvious she would like to get to know him better. Ezra thought she might be fun, but had the feeling she was looking for a husband, not a weekend between the sheets.

Ezra left for Eurydice with a long list of supplies for the farm and his books. The road to his farm had been improved and without having to drag a train of equipment behind him, he made the trip in four hours and checked into the hotel.

He went to place his orders so they would be ready when he finished with the Settler's Office, then bought work clothing for himself and the men.

That evening as he was taking his dinner, he noticed three men across the small dining room that acted unusual for the way they were dressed. They were dressed business like but acted more like sailors on liberty. The sanitary facilities were behind them and Ezra decided to make use of them in order to get a closer look at the men. What he saw almost tied a knot in his stomach as one man had a tattoo on his left hand which matched tattoos found on Denali Rangers.

What were Rangers doing in Eurydice?

As he was exiting the facilities he witnessed one of the men being crude to Betty, the waitress. His language was one thing, but his hands were another. Ezra never thought as he acted on the situation.

The man was rubbing Betty's leg as she was trying to serve their orders. Ezra stepped to them, grabbed the man's wrist and flipped him out of his chair. With his other hand, he gently moved Betty out of the way as he spoke to the man now on the floor.

"Mister, keep your hands to yourself, but if you have to play with someone's leg, I bet your buddy would like it."

The fight that started ended nearly as fast. Ezra did take a hit to his jaw, but his full beard softened the blow and he dropped that man with a punch to the throat. The man on the floor was coming up with a knife in hand when Ezra kicked him in the chin which drove the back of his head into the wall behind him, knocking him out. The third man made it more interesting as he was standing with a knife in hand, but Ezra scooped up a plate of hot food off the table and just flipped it up into the man's face.

Ezra then grabbed the heavy glass water pitcher off the table and hit him in the face with it, dropping him like a sack of potatoes.

He looked at the three men to insure they were not going to be any more trouble before turning to Betty.

"Betty, call the Marshalls please."

She just looked at him then ran back to the service counter for the communicator. After she disconnected the call, she told Ezra the Marshalls were on their way, then she sat down on one of the stools along the counter as Ezra just stepped further back and waited.

It took less than five minutes for the Marshalls to arrive and they went directly to Betty. She told them about the man getting fresh with her, then Ezra coming to her rescue. One of the Marshalls came to Ezra as the other checked on the men on the floor. Ezra showed him his papers and told him what had happened from his point of view and that no man had a right to lay hands on a woman in such a manner, especially in a café.

"Well Mister Connors, it looks like you've had some experience in dealing with men in this manner."

"I worked as a bouncer in a bar on Watkins for a while. But are their Lancers at the Federation Embassy?"

"Sure, there are a dozen, why?"

"I think you had best get them involved. That man there has a tattoo on his left hand similar to those worn by Denali's Rangers. The Lancers might be interested to know if they all have that tattoo and if they do, what they are doing on Nemea."

"How come you know about those tattoos?"

"I was working on Buckner during the rebellion when those Rangers showed up. I got out of the way as quick as I could before it dropped in the pot."

The Marshall gave Ezra a look that was somewhere between sure, I believe you and you're full of crap at the same time. The Marshall radioed his office for them to contact the Lancers and have someone to come to the café to confirm Ezra's statement about the tattoos. Every Law Enforcement agency throughout the Federation had been instructed to notify Federation authorities if they had contact with a Ranger, regardless of the situation.

An aircar arrived ten minutes later and two Lancers entered the café armed for combat. Ezra gave an internal sigh of relief in that he did not recognize either of the men, and with his full beard and long hair tied back into a ponytail, he figured nature had given him a decent disguise.

The Lancer Sergeant grabbed the wrist of the first man he came too, then flipped him over on his face and put a knee in his back even though the man was still unconscious. He pulled restraints from his leg pouch and put the on the man then moved to the next and repeated the process. Soon they were all restrained as they were slowly becoming conscious.

The Marshall and Sergeant talked for a minute then the Sergeant turned to Ezra.

"The Marshall tells me you were on Buckner during the rebellion. What were you doing there?"

"Operating a scraper in the copper mines."

The Sergeant nodded his head.

"I was in on that fight. I went down with the First of the Seventh Lancers. We'll take these folks with us and see if they can tell us what they are doing here."

"Sergeant," Ezra spoke up again. "These men owe the café for their meals."

The Sergeant smiled, kneeled down and rolled the man over and went through his pockets. Then he went from man to man collecting their cash money. He had nearly a hundred Federation Crowns in hand when he walked over to Betty.

"Ma'am, cash those men out and put the rest in your pocket as payment for their rudeness. They're not going to need any money where they are going.

That evening Betty knocked on Ezra's door and this time, he did not turn her away. She made it clear entering the room that she had no intention of getting into a relationship, but after the events earlier in the day, they both need some stress relief. Betty was thirty-three and a widow who knew her way around a bed. She left his room just after midnight for her own.

Slight Complications

Ezra was ushered into the office of one Hiram Greeson, the Federation's office manager of the Settlement Office. This was an informal meeting prior to Ezra's audit.

"Mister Connors, thank you for coming in today as I understand you are very busy at your farm."

"Mister Greeson, according to Federation Regulations, I have no choice but to be here, so here I am."

"Yes, well, we shall try to make this as painless as possible for you. Miss Wetherspoon will be handling your audit today."

"Mister Greeson, did you specifically assign Miss Wetherspoon to be my auditor?"

"No. When she saw the audit list, she volunteered to handle your audit. Why?"

"Are you aware her brother, Simon works for me. Now please understand I am sure Miss Wetherspoon will do a thorough job of my audit but if there is a tiny mistake in the books that I have missed, and let's say she also misses it. An honest mistake of course. It could look poorly on her and this office if the Federation Auditing Office catches the mistake when I submit my taxes. Someone with a sharp pencil might think there was something going on between the young lady and myself since her brother is clearly reported as my employee."

"Oh, I see your point Mister Connors. Susanne, Miss Wetherspoon is a fine employee, but we are all human and mistakes can happen. Yes, I'll reassign your case to Mister Ponder."

"Thank you Mister Greeson. I was just thinking about the reputation of your office, Sir."

Mister Ponder held the appearance of the typical bureaucrat in that he was short, overweight, and balding. He went right to work on Ezra's books checking then rechecking entries comparing

37

them to invoices and receipts before moving to the next entry. When he commented there was no invoice on an entry, Ezra told him he could not find the invoice and forgot to request a copy from the vendor, but it was small enough he was not concerned about the taxes.

Ponder just shook his head and told Ezra that the Crowns that were paid in taxes were Crowns he could not spend on Nemea or pay an employee, then he contacted the vendor and asked for a copy of the invoice for record. It arrived within five minutes by electronic means and was placed in the books, zeroing out that entry.

Ezra only smiled as the taxes would have only amounted to a couple of Crowns and he had the invoice in his pocket. He was wanting to see just how thorough the audit would be.

When the lunch period arrived, Ponder took a sandwich from his desk and told Ezra he always ate at the office and today he would work as he ate in hope of finishing the audit today so Ezra could return to his farm. But there was no need for Ezra to miss the mid-day meal and if there were any questions while he was gone to eat, he'd just make a note of them for when he returned.

He had just left the building when he heard his name called out from behind him. Ezra felt he knew the voice and was not surprised when he turned back to see Susanne Wetherspoon walking towards him.

"Mister Connors, are you taking lunch?"

"Yes Miss Wetherspoon, I am."

"May I walk with you? I'm eating at the café today?"

"How interesting so am I since I'm staying at the hotel. Certain, you may walk with me, but answer me this. Why did you volunteer to audit my books?"

She smiled before answering.

"Am I that obvious?"

"Yes Miss Wetherspoon, you are. Before we take another step let me say this. You are an attractive young lady and the thirteen years between us is not a problem for me, but the problem is I am your brother's employer, and you work for the Settler's Office. Unless I am grossly mistaken you are looking for a serious relationship, romance which is normal for a woman of any age, but look elsewhere Miss Wetherspoon because I am not interested."

"And you have no interest in a night in your bed?" She asked him.

"Miss Wetherspoon, Susanne, that statement disappoints me when considering your character and I am going to pretend you never spoke it."

He started to turn away from her until she grabbed his arm.

"Mister Connors, Ezra, the number on my Nemea Birth record is three. I lost my virginity when I was fourteen to a man older than you are now, and I do not regret it at all. If it wasn't for the Hanover Foundation I would have never been able to go to New Brumsfield for the university. I've heard dozens of stories from Simon about you and yes, I would like to see if a romance could develop between us, but I am neither naïve or stupid to think I can screw you to the altar. But as you mentioned, in my position, I must be very careful whom I sleep with. From what Simon has said about you, I doubt if I would have risked much other than enjoying the time together. Good Day Mister Connors."

Ezra watched as she walked away from him, heading towards another eatery. For a moment he considered following her then just smiled, and went to the café at the hotel.

In the café he noticed a Marshall sitting at the bar, drinking a cup of coffee or tea, just ignoring everyone, but was positioned so he could see the entire café. Ezra just smiled and took a table where he could also watch the café as he ate.

Back in the Settler's Office after lunch, Ezra just sat and watched Ponder run the numbers in his books until mid-afternoon when he closed the books and smiled at Ezra.

"Mister Connors, whomever taught you to keep records did an excellent job of it. I find nothing wrong with your books and even with the start-up expenditures of starting up the farm, you are showing a nice profit. It is fortunate that there is a need for your hay off world."

"Yes Mister Ponder, there is no doubt I got lucky there, otherwise I'd be lucky to break even this first year."

"Yes, you were. Any plans for the future the Office can help you with?"

"I was wondering about the track of land South on my place. Is it spoken for?"

"Let me look."

Ponder left the office for a few minutes to check the Settler's map of the planet to see if they land was already allocated. He returned with good news for Ezra.

"No Mister Connors. It was once allocated but the settler could not make a go of it and forfeited the claim. Would you care to make a claim on it? The section is roughly thirty-two hundred hectares."

"Then how about we get the paperwork moving on my taking claim on the land. I'm considering doing some clearing and processing the trees into lumber."

"Well that is an expensive endeavor Mister Connors."

"Yes, but what you audited was the farm account. I still have my personal accounts which can handle the outlay. I need to build a couple bridges across the creeks on my land, and there are plenty of trees to mill for that project. But I will replant in those areas I will not be farming later."

"Well then, let me get the forms and get this going for you."

Two hours later the paperwork was done and Ezra had signed the authorization for paying the fees via the Federation's Exchequer where his primary account was being kept for him. When Ponder saw the account data he gave Ezra a questioning look but did not venture to ask how he had an account with the Exchequer.

When Ezra entered the café for the evening meal, he saw the Lancer Sergeant sitting in a far corner who waved for him to join him. Ezra pulled up a chair where he could also see the café and sat down.

"What can I do for you Sergeant Murphy?"

"Please, just call me Kendall. Now Mister Connors, this café has a surveillance video installed and after you left us yesterday, I took a look at the video with the Marshall. You said you were a bouncer at one time and that sort of fits, but I have never seen a bouncer with the smoothness you displayed, but I have seen Marines and Lancers display such technique. But the interesting thing is your name does not pop-up in the computers as ever being a Marine or Lancer. Not even in the Fleet."

"Well Kendall, what if I told you my teacher who taught me to be a bouncer was a former Lancer, would that make you happy? And call me Ezra."

Kendall laughed.

"Yeah Ezra, I'll put that in my contact report tonight. Now the Rangers you handed over to us are off planet, heading to out Psych Docs to drain them of any and all information possible. We cleaned out their rooms and found some very interesting things tucked away in them. Still do not know why they were here, but underneath the table is a satchel containing a few items that we Lancers feel you may need. And I suspect you know how to use them."

"I think I can muddle through understanding the operational concepts of the items."

Once more Kendal laughed as he stood.

"One last thing. A section of Marines dropped on your farm last night. If they're worth a damn you'll never see them, but they will be there until we get this figured out. Those damn Rangers are bad about hitting back at those that kick their ass. The public record shows all you did was defend Betty's honor as they were trying to molest her. The Marshall's office is taking the heat for turning them over to the Federation based on an open Federation warrant against the Denali Rangers. A section of Marines dropped on the town last night also and two sections of Lancers will be on the ground tonight. Sleep easy Ezra as we are watching the hotel."

"Betty?"

"We have her covered also."

"Thanks."

As soon as Kendall left, Betty came over to take his order. She told him that Kendall had asked her to stay away while they talked and so she waited until then. After dinner Ezra took the satchel to his room to find out what the Lancers had provided him.

The satchel contained a ten millimeter pistol with five loaded magazines, a Marine's trench knife, and lightweight body armor that he could wear under his clothing without giving away he was protected. The pistol also came with a shoulder holster which was of civilian use, not service usage.

Ezra tore the pistol down and checked each piece before reassembling and making it ready if needed. He did not expect Betty to return to his bed tonight, but when she knocked on his door, he just went with the flow and they fell asleep in each other's arms.

The Next Step

Ezra left Eurydice just before noon loaded with the supplies he had ordered and the paperwork for the new land, plus invoices for the saw mill equipment that would be delivered the next week. He wasn't sure, but felt there was a cloaked Assault Boat covering his journey to the farm. Even if Kendall suspected Ezra had once been a Lancer, the Lancers were noted for taking care of those who assisted in the work they did.

Two weeks after Ezra returned to the farm, he was watching as the first pieces of lumber were coming off the saw when an air car landed near the saw mill. It was an armored air car and from it, Kendall exited and walked over to him.

"Kendall, what can I do for you?" Ezra said in greeting as he offered his hand to him.

"Ezra, just came to tell you those Rangers were only passing through the area. They had a layover, changing transports when they collided with you. On the plus side, the information they provided led us to where they were going and why. Roger Denali, their leader is now heading for the iron mines on Denoyelles. Marines took him and his entire staff during a raid."

"That's certainly good news. Now those Marines hiding in my timber can go back to doing some real work."

Kendall grinned.

"Yeah, they'll pull out tonight once everyone has called it a day. Anyway, thanks for what bit of service you provided in removing the Rangers. The universe is a safer place with Denali and his crew out of action."

"Kendall, we both know it was pure luck, and that's all. Karma put us all in the same place at the right time. If that one man had not try to molest Betty, no telling what would have happened."

Kendall nodded his head, offered his hand and left Ezra thinking he should have done something, just what he didn't know.

He just let that thought exit his mind and turned back to the saw mill.

Ezra watched the mill work for over an hour thinking he was lucky to find an older man, semi-retired that knew how to operate a saw mill and had convinced him to teach his hands how to operate the mill and produce lumber. As the boards were coming out of the mill, they were going to a stack to air dry, then in a couple of months, they would be used to build new quarters for his hands, especially the married ones so they could bring their wives to live on the farm.

He checked his chronometer and decided it was time to go to the area they were cutting the trees and teach Simon and the others how to place the charges to blow the stumps as they were clearing the ground for future planting of a food crop, specifically wheat.

There was a bit of irony to what was happening to Ezra and his plans to disappear into the universe. He sat looking at the large map on his office wall of his farm thinking how to further improve his situation. He now had twenty-two employees and figured another ten minimum to move things further along.

He remembered the lessons from his parents to get the most out of the land without damaging it. A deal had been made with a rancher on the far side of the continent for a bull and fifty head of beef cattle to start a small ranching operation on five hundred hectares he had fences off. The first of the cattle was to arrive within the week.

Ezra was also considering fencing off another five hundred hectares and stocking it with dairy cattle to provide milk to his hands and the few children moving onto the place. Also once up and running, his dairy would be closer to Eurydice than the ones that was supplying the town.

Orders for hay had jumped because of planets having droughts besides the one he was already supplying. Ezra never hesitated to send those buyers to the other farms to fill the contracts and in doing so developed a solid relationship with his competitors in the business. The other farmer's followed his business model in pricing so everyone would profit without the competition between farms.

Now three months into his expansion he was finding himself needing more hands yet the labor force was dwindling quick with the other farms hiring to meet their needs. He also had discovered an outcropping of limestone in the new ground covering about two hundred hectares that he figured he could quarry for various things, especially gravel for his own roads. But he needed experienced people for that job. But he knew right where to go to get the help.

Ezra went to Eurydice with one thing on his mind, and that was to talk to the Lancers about them finding retired Lancer Combat Engineers to come and work for him. They knew explosives, heavy equipment, and more importantly how not to kill themselves doing such work.

He sat down with the Lancers and spelled out what he needed, hedging it some so it would not sound like he had first hand knowledge of the abilities of Lancer Engineers. He said he knew they had Engineers and figured they could handle the work better than people that had very little if any background in the work. The Lancers agreed to put out a call for a dozen men with specific qualifications on their Uni-Web site for him.

As an after-thought, he went by the Settler's Office and found Susanne in her office doing paperwork. He gently rapped on her open door to get her attention.

"Yes, Mister Connors, can I help you?"

"I was wondering if your were free for dinner tonight?"

"After our last conversation, I figured you would consider me a waste of time."

"Time is this evening, say seven? Beyond that is out of my control."

"And what if I want more, say around nine?"

"As I said, that is out of my control."

"Then I shall see you at seven.   Good Day Mister Connors."

Ezra spent the rest of the day placing orders for equipment and other goods for the farm. He knew he was eating deeply into his base account but the knowledge it would get somewhat refreshed every three months made it easier to spend. He was betting on a future he had not planned for and the money actually meant nothing more than he could survive when others failed. But he had to succeed or all the time and energy was just a waste.

Betty had came to him during lunch and told him that she had been seeing one of the Lancers so he was not to expect her at his door tonight. He told her he was glad she may have found a good man and from everything he had heard, Lancers were good men.

Susanne arrived exactly at seven dressed as she did for work. The conversation was a bit awkward at first, then she loosened up as dinner progressed. By eight forty-five, she was ripping the skin off his back, and telling the Saints how grand her night was. An hour later she revived him and they repeated before both fell asleep.

Ezra woke her up in plenty of time to go home and change for the day. She asked him to stay another night and have dinner at her place. He had already made plans to meet with a gentleman who ran a dairy far from Eurydice which provided milk to several of the outlaying settlements for the purchase of a minimum of a dozen head of dairy cows. They closed the deal at twenty head and the assurance the bull he had already bought could service the cows and they would still provide plenty of milk and in some cases make stronger cows. Any bulls from the breeding could either be kept as a breeder or cut for steers and grown for beef.

The last thing he did before meeting with Susanne was to order an air car so he could get around the planet quicker than the old truck that was needed more on the farm than taking him around to conduct business. Tonight was a repeat of the previous evening except it started with her laying on the dinner table before it was every cleared of the dishes.

As Ezra was exhausting himself with Susanne, three Lancers stopped two armed men who were sneaking up the back stairs to Susanne's apartment. Neither men had the tattoos of the Rangers, but it would be later discovered they were contract killers with detain and hold warrants against them from five other planetary systems in relation to unsolved murders in those systems.

Ezra returned to his room just before daylight to find Kendall Murphy sitting in his room waiting for him.

"Sergeant Murphy, is there a reason you are in my room at this hour?"

"Well, I didn't think it would be proper to bother you in Miss Wetherspoon's apartment. I must say she is an attractive woman and very selective in her playmates. But what I am here about is the two men that were following you yesterday."

"Yeah, what about them? Is there a reason you are having me followed?"

Kendall laughed.

"Ezra, you're slipping. Those weren't Lancers, they were contract killers, and guess who the contract is on?"

Ezra took his light jacket off, then the shoulder holster for the pistol Kendall had given him.

"Well, to be honest I wasn't sure who they were and this was never out of reach."

"Never?"

"Never. Now what do you know about the contract?"

"Not much. Intelligence caught wind of it about a month ago. You're being blamed for Denali's capture and of the three men you took out, two are dead, and the other is in isolation now to protect him. It seems the Rangers are wanting payment for your pissing in their cereal."

"What's the plan now?"

"That's what I'd like to know too. You see every time we try to do a back ground on you, it gets hung up further up the line. Now that tells me that either Lancer Intelligence or Fleet Intelligence, maybe both, are involved. Then there is the fact you are financially better off then the average settler. Shall I continue with my theory?"

"No, but let me give you one of my own. Your rank is of a junior Sergeant, yet with a Senior Sergeant and Lieutenant at the Embassy, you are doing all of the leg work on this. The Intelligence work. Your also talking about accessing information that is far above your pay grade. Then the small detail that you're better educated than the average Sergeant. So, what are you? A Captain or Major in Lancer Intelligence, and what are you doing on Nemea in disguise."

Kendall stood and walked past Ezra to the door.

"Mister Connors, if the Fleet and Lancer Headquarters are covering your ass, it is for a reason which I shall never know unless you tell me. And I'm smart enough not to ask that question of you. Now a bit of information you need to know. Within a week, you'll have a full section of Lancer Engineers at your farm to deal with the work you will publicly hire them for. They're not retirees, but line Engineers. Also a full section of Infantry will show up also as hired help. All of them have farm experience. I'm sure you can find a way to make it look as if you are running split shifts on the farm giving the grunts a chance to cover your ass. Watch your six Mister Connors, someone wants to put a bullet in it and right now, we don't know who."

With that he exited Ezra's room giving him something to consider. With the capture of Denali and his staff there were a lot of Rangers out of work and they were not noted for their logic. Could one or more be trying to pay him back for being out of work? If two of the men he took out and turned over to the

Lancers were now dead, coming after him was a serious possibility.

One Point Seven Meters of Trouble

Ezra was concerned that he was about to lose control of his own life considering that the day after he asked for retired Lancers to come work for him, he was told he was getting a full section of Combat Engineers instead plus a section of Infantry.

Karma was one thing, but were the Fates playing dice with his life? As with many who once flew amongst the stars, Ezra was not superstitious, but there were things in the Universe which could not be explained with science.

The Engineers arrived on what appeared to be a commercial freighter with the equipment he supposedly ordered to open a rock quarry and crusher site. They landed at the Eurydice Space Port and brought two air cars with them with the paperwork showing he had ordered them. Ezra was also handed a plain envelope with a letter telling him that all of the quarry and logging equipment he had received was paid for, and to use it as needed. The letter was hand written and had no signature, but he knew where it came from even if the Engineer would never tell him how he came by it.

The Lancer Captain who was in charge of the Engineers had Ezra take him out to where he wanted the operation set up then had the freighter land on site so they could unload the equipment where it needed to be instead of having to truck it to the site.

A week later a transport arrived with the Infantry Section plus a couple of extra people. Again it looked like a standard transport but like the freighter, it was a special purpose Lancer transport disguised as a commercial transport. They were off loaded at Eurydice and rented trucks transported them and their baggage to the farm. Here is where trouble struck for Ezra.

The Infantry Section Leader handed Ezra a roster of personal which he just glanced at before going out to meet the new people. It was there he took a hard look at the roster and realized he knew one of them even if their name was now different.

The roster showed two females who were to be assigned to his house as cook and housekeepers. One name was Clare Montfort. His mind was racing as Cherry had married a man named Montfort, and this could not be a coincidence. He looked the group over and indeed one of the females in civilian clothing was a redhead, but she was not a Centaurian. Regardless of her lack of body and facial fur, it was Cherry. The other female was a dark skinned individual named Regina Bloomfield. He addressed the group.

"Ladies, gentlemen welcome to my farm. I'm Ezra Connors. Gentlemen, your quarters are behind the house. The blue building was completed yesterday for you so if you go get yourself situated, we can worry about assignments tomorrow. Ladies, there are rooms in the house for you since that is where you will be working. Please go find a room and we'll talk more later as I need to go out and check on a few things. Dismissed."

He just stood in place as the two females walked past him with Cherry/Clare moving past him without looking at him. Ezra breathed a sigh of relief in that either she did not recognize him or she was keeping his secret, but either way, he saw her as trouble in the long run. But if she was here, where was her husband?

Ezra went out to the timber cutting operation to see how the new tree cutting equipment was working out. He went from there to the quarry before stopping and checking on the baling. He was postponing going home as long as he could because he was uncertain how to deal with Clare.

He found both women sitting in is living room when he walked into the house. Both stood as he entered.

"Please be seated ladies, let's keep this as informal as possible. Now who does what here?"

"Mister Connors, we double up. Both of us will work as cooks and housekeepers." It was Regina who spoke up.

"Well that's up to you, but I did not request either of you so I'll try to stay out of your way as much as possible. If there is anything you need, please let me know."

It was Clare who responded next.

"Mister Connors, Regina and I are both experienced Lancers. We have been positioned here to protect you within your quarters. Cooking for you and keeping your house is only a cover Sir. But I think you'll find both of use will be more than adequate in both our cover and in protecting you, Sir."

"Well then I think we have covered this as well as we can at the moment. I'll be in my office so you can familiarize yourself with the house and the pantry. Oh, and if you wish something special for the pantry, please make a list and we'll order it."

Ezra went to his office and left the door open as he hoped they would see him busy and not disturb him. It didn't work. Ten minutes later Clare walked into his office and closed the door behind her, then leaned back against it.

"What am I to call you?" She asked.

"Ezra is my name, Clare."

"Ezra, I honestly did not know it was you when they asked for volunteers, or I would not be here."

"Clare, I heard you were married."

"Widowed is the proper term now Ezra."

"Clare, I am truly sorry to hear that."

"It's been nearly a year now, but I only want to say it is good to see you again. Now having said that I'm going to tell Lieutenant Steinfeld that I need to be replaced on the detail."

"Was my name, this name mentioned when you volunteered?"

"Yes, it was."

"Then how are you going to explain the need to be reassigned without giving away who I once was?"

Tears began rolling down her cheeks.

"Damn it Eli, I mean Ezra. I've only loved two men in my life. One is now dead and the other is looking at me knowing this is wrong and it can never work. Not like this."

"No, It can't work. But what happened to your lovely fur?"

"When I met Stephen, I had gone through a temporary removal for an assignment. We had made love several times by the time my fur began returning and to be honest, I really enjoyed the feeling of flesh to flesh. I had it permanently removed before the wedding. I really don't miss it."

Ezra put his elbows on his desk, then cupped his head in his hands as he was trying to figure out how to handle this without either of them getting hurt.

"Ezra, I haven't been with a man since Stephen died. This is all wrong but right now, all I can think of is the times we spent together."

"Clare, I'm lost here too. But if you back out of this you might as well leave the Lancers as they will never give you another undercover assignment. You'll find yourself doing shit details until you resign."

She just stood, shaking as she cried. Ezra remembered how tough she once was, fearless as she defused an IED, or under fire. No fearless was the wrong word, brave was more like it. What happened to her to make her like this now? He stood and moved from his desk to her, took her in his arms and pulled her close.

"Clare, I've missed you, but every bone in my body says this is going to end badly, and I don't want that. Besides, what do we tell Regina?"

Clare composed herself, and spoke without looking up at him.

"Before I came in here, I told her that you and I once had a relationship, years ago, and I volunteered for this assignment thinking if it was in fact you, that maybe we could reignite those old feelings, even for a short time. That was a lie of course because I didn't know it was you until you spoke to us outside. The beard and hair hides you very well, but I can never forget your voice."

"Then we better get our stories straight. There is a Lancer Intelligence Officer masquerading as a Sergeant at the Embassy that already suspects my background is a false front. If you say the wrong thing, it can cause both of us trouble."

He pulled her head back, leaned down to her and kissed her feeling her pent-up passion releasing into her return kiss. She wrapped her arms around him and he could fell her fingers digging into his back through his shirt. This was wrong, but he knew it felt the way things should be.

When they finally broke the kiss, he sat her down on the couch in his office and they went over the story she would tell if questioned about their relationship. It followed the back story he had memorized that the Fleet had given this name and it flowed well enough with her own history that it was as believable as possible.

That night in bed, they rekindled feelings that they once had to conceal, hide from others even at the expense of taking others to bed.

During the day, Ezra and Clare kept their distance, playing the game for all to see, even if Regina just smiled at the interaction knowing that once the day was done, where they would end up. The fact Clare was there to protect him from harm was made easy by the fact she and Regina set intrusion devices at every location that could be used to enter the house with receivers in every utilized bedroom.

The Engineers soon had the quarry in operation, crushing limestone into gravel and building roads through and around the farm. Once that was complete, they began to gravel the road from

54

the farm to Eurydice, laying heavy stone down, packing it in then a small gravel to level the surface.

The Lancers and Ezra's farm employees mixed well as the Lancers only commented they had done time in service and was now just trying to make a living. Since payroll was automated, the hands never knew the Lancers were being paid much more money than they were receiving for doing the same work. At night, the Lancers would maintain two hour patrol shifts in order to give everyone a decent amount of rest plus they had also installed intrusion detection devices around the farm house area, further out making the patrols much easier on all concerned.

One Lancer commented to another that this duty was much easier than some they stood. He was told to remember why they were there and not to get complacent. Regina also had to remind Clare of the same thing even after Regina hooked up with one of the Nemean's that worked in the dairy.

Ezra was eating guilt as he was making money, yet over half his labor force were not physically on his payroll. The orders for hay had leveled out with the next five cuttings already spoken for along with having to put hay back for his own use.

Once he had all the buildings, quarters built, he now had lumber in excess. But he had several hundred hectares of land he needed cleared for farming and he was not about to just clear cut and burn the timber. He put the word out that he had lumber from heavy beams for bridging, to trim boards to use on the interior of a house.

There were two other lumber operations on the planet but the lumber yards made a deal to buy ten percent of his stock lumber plus he was to cut special measures on call which the other mills would not do. Also there was a panel company which bought his waste chips and saw dust to make what they called particle boards and whole logs to peel for making plywood.

Ezra looked at the lumber industry on the planet and discovered no one was compressing saw dust for fire logs or making barbecue bricks. He found a supplier of machinery to

55

compress the saw dust and chips to make those items and expanded that part of the business.

Six months after the Lancers had arrived, Ezra looked at his books and could only shake his head. How was he going to explain the massive increase in income to the Auditing Office without the labor cost expenditures, plus the equipment?

He came to Nemea to hide from the universe and found himself known over nearly a third of it because of his supplying hay, a common farm item, to planets suffering with drought so they could maintain their cattle enterprises so they could feed their populations.

On his desk was an order for heavy timbers from the Fleet for use in various construction projects. The order came in without a request for bids telling him someone was feeding him orders without regard to protocol. But the price for the timbers were in line with what he could find on the web. He was tempted to no charge the invoices for the timbers, but also knew that would raise eyebrows which would lead to questions he did not need to try to answer.

Then there was Clare. As comfortable life had became with her, they both knew it would have to eventually end. She had even brought up the subject one night in bed that they were too much alike and eventually that would wear on their relationship.

He never asked her how her husband had died, nor had he looked it up on the Lancer Web, but he could tell that experience had changed her in ways she was still fighting deep inside. And nothing in his life or training had taught him how to help her beyond what was happening between them. Ezra resigned himself to just letting their relationship move along the path the Fates had determined for them.

A Warning Too Late

It was nearly eight months into their affair that the end came during the night. The Lancers were receiving intelligence briefings almost daily but there was an old saying that went, if you thank you have enough intelligence, then you are missing something. What they were missing were the events of the night.

During the night a transport entered low orbit around Nemea, discharging two small shuttles which dropped on the farm. The night watch barely got the alarm out as over a dozen armed men erupted out of each shuttle attacking the house.

The first attacker to gain entrance into the house was blown back out the door by Regina with a cut-down shotgun as Ezra and Clare just put on enough clothes before grabbing their weapons kept on a small table by the bedroom door.

The fight was centered on the house as the attackers were firing at the windows without knowing they had been replaced months before by bullet resistant glass. Regina had moved to the door, taking a position beside it and firing when she had a target. Clare joined her on the opposite side watching the other angle to the door. Ezra threw up a heavy table across the living room from the door and watched for anyone pressing entrance into the house.

The fight outside took a new direction as the Lancers were responding to the attack. There was an explosion at the rear of the house which caused Ezra to turn towards that direction and took out two attackers that had gained access after blowing the back door open. He watched the back of the house until a Lancer entered and took up position to cover the door, then another Lancer arrived, moving through the house to the front door.

When Ezra turned back to the front, he quickly noticed that Clare was no longer standing by the door. It only took a moment to find her, lying on the floor, crumpled up, unmoving. Then as suddenly as the fire fight started, a deathly silence fell over the farm.

Ezra moved to Clare's body to see blood on her head, and a piece of her scalp missing. He checked her pulse at her neck, with it telling him she was still alive from the head wound she had received.

"I've called for a Medic boss." The Lancer at the door informed him.

"Thanks." He knew there was nothing he could do for her as he looked across at Regina who was applying a bandage to her left arm.

"Regina, how bad is it?" He called over to her.

"Just a graze, I'll be alright."

They heard a call that a medic was coming in, and seconds later a Lancer Medic entered the door, looked around, then went down by Clare and carefully checked her out before applying a bandage to her head to help seal the wound. He pulled an IV system from his bag, and started her on replacement fluids, handing the bag to the Lancer still standing by the door.

Lieutenant Steinfeld entered the house, just standing at the door looking at Ezra then Clare. He turned back and called for a litter before addressing Ezra.

"Mister Connors, are you alright?"

"Yeah Lieutenant, but Regina took a light hit. How's your people?"

"I have one dead, and three wounded not counting Clare. We took five prisoners and still getting a headcount on their dead. I'm sorry Mister Connors, but we didn't get a warning until they were nearly on the ground."

"I understand Lieutenant. Go see to your people."

Ezra stood, looked back down at Clare, then went to his office where he removed a bottle of Hayutan Whisky from his desk and just pulled the cork from it, taking a long drink directly from the bottle. He sat for a time then looked at the bottle and replaced the cork. Whisky was not the answer to the pain he was feeling inside.

There was a rap on his door.

"Mister Connors, there is a Fleet Cruiser three hours out. As soon as we can, we're going to lift Clare and the other wounded so they can receive treatment. Our medic thinks Clare will be alright but she'll be down for some time."

"Three hours out?"

"Yes Sir. It seems they were chasing the transport that brought those folks here. We just got the word late."

"Interesting. Do you know Sergeant Murphy at the Embassy?"

"Yes Sir, I do."

"Send a team to collect him before that Cruiser gets here. I wish to talk to him."

Steinfeld looked at Ezra for a moment then nodded before leaving to execute his orders.

It was over an hour later that the air car sent to collect Murphy returned with him upset about being drug out of the Embassy in the middle of the night. His escorts took him to Ezra's office then left him alone with Ezra when he dismissed them. The anger Murphy had entering the office was mellowed when he saw Ezra sitting behind his desk with the pistol he had been given on top of it.

"Kendall, I have four wounded Lancers and a dead one on my conscious right now. I have been informed that there was a cruiser chasing the transport that brought those men to kill me. Now I would like to think that you never received any notice of that chase, but all I have to do is place an interstellar call to know the truth. Did you know they were coming after me?"

"Yes, I was notified last night."

"Before they gained orbit?"

"Yes."

"Do you want to tell me why I don't just kill you where you stand for keeping that information from the Lancers that are here to protect me?"

"I didn't think they'd attack so quickly."

"Kendall, let me explain something to you. Who I once was, and who wants to keep me alive can insure that you spend the rest of your life cleaning latrines in the iron mines on Denoyelles because of your incompetence in this matter."

Ezra stood and walked around his desk to stand nearly nose to nose with Murphy.

"I once wore the rank of a Fleet Full Commander. I've lost people in battle, but never, and I mean never was I denied the tiniest bit of Intelligence where an opponent was concerned. The death of a Lancer lies at your feet as does the blood of the injured Lancers. Here is the deal I will make you and you have no choice in the matter. I shall stay quiet and you will leave Nemea on the cruiser in bound here. Also you will never speak to anyone about what I have said here tonight."

Ezra stepped around Murphy and called out to the Corporal who had brought him to the farm.

"Corporal, escort Sergeant Murphy back to the Embassy, insure he gets his bags packed and bring him back here to lift to the cruiser with the prisoners. If he gives you any trouble, cuff him and gag him if necessary."

"Yes Sir Mister Connors. Let's go Murphy."

As soon as the detail left with Murphy, Regina showed up with a mug of coffee for Ezra.

"Thanks Regina."

"Ezra, she'll make it."

"I know Regina. We both knew that what we have had could not last, but this was not a good way to end it."

"Actually it is. This way there is no awkward words between the two of you. She told me that when the assignment was over, she was lifting with the rest of us. She also told me she was scared of that time as she had no idea what or how to tell you she was leaving."

"Thanks Regina, that was actually comforting. What about you? What are your plans?"

"Buck asked me to marry him."

"And?"

"I'm thinking about it. Seeing Clare lying there and the wound I took makes me think I've pushed my luck as far as I can."

"Was he aware you are a Lancer?"

"No, but he just left the house and is okay with who I really am."

"Then let me sweeten the pot. If you marry Buck, I'll hire you to stay as my cook and housekeeper."

"I'll think about it. Thanks."

She left him to just wait, thinking he should go see Clare before she lifted but knew if he did, his anger would return and this time he might not be able to contain it.

He stood on the porch as the shuttle with Clare on board lifted for the cruiser as the second shuttle was loading with Murphy and the prisoners. Off to the side were the bodies of the dead, laid out with their equipment piled up in front of them. The two shuttles that brought them down were sitting in the early morning sun, both with blood on their ramps and the scars of bullets on their hulls.

Word had came down from space that the transport had tried to slip away when the attack failed, but two Fast Destroyer's that were with the Cruiser quickly ran it down with a section of Marines boarding the vessel.

The Lancers at the quarry had came up to assist in any manner they could, and the farm hands were mixing with the Lancers now having learned who they really were. Ezra was glad to know that when the shooting started, the farm hands just hunkered down and stayed out of the way.

The bodies were being stripped of all clothing and photographed for tattoos and other identifying marks along with fingerprints and DNA. Another team was going through the shuttles, insuring there was nothing in them to be a danger. These raiders had came down complete with the shuttle pilots being part of the actual raid and were now dead or captured.

Lieutenant Steinfeld walked over to Ezra as the bodies were being processed.

"Mister Connors, what do you want us to do with the bodies?"

"Lieutenant, have the Engineers cut a deep trench and dump them in it, then cover it up with slabs of limestone with a Bio-Hazard Warning sign on it. There's a spot at the far back of the property that would be a good place to put them."

"Yes, Sir, I'll get with Captain Mercer and arrange that right now Sir."

Ezra told his farm hands to take the day off and only deal with things that could not be put aside such as milking and feeding the cows.

When he went back into the house, he noticed the smell of disinfectant, then the spot where Clare had been laying was now clear of blood. The door frame would have to be replaced as it took several hits as did the walls inside the living room. Furniture had been shot up and the windows, although bullet resistant, were now scarred from bullet impacts.

Moving to the rear of the house he found Regina cleaning up the mess from the two men he had killed there, plus the fragments of the door and frame when they blew it open. He asked her if she had eaten and when she said no, he told her to continue with what she was doing and he'd fix them both something to eat. They sat in silence as they ate, neither wishing to talk about the night.

Late in the afternoon, they received word that Clare was in good shape after surgery to take some pressure off her brain and it was felt she should recover without any disability. She was going to be taken to Zyra, her home world to rest and recover.

That night as he lay in bed, a shadow from the door came over him. He slowly rose up to see Regina standing in the doorway, backlighted by the hallway light, her shape outlined inside her pale nightgown.

"Yes Regina?"

"I'm going to marry Buck, and yes, I'll take care of your house and cook for you. We can discuss wages in the morning, but I wanted you to know this tonight."

"Alright Regina, thank you. Pleasant dreams."

"Good Night Ezra."

Services Rendered

Five days after the fight, Ezra was contacted by the Federation Embassy and asked to come to Eurydice to meet with the Ambassador. Actually he was asked to meet at the Space Port.

Against his wishes, he flew with a Lancer pilot along with two other aircars flown by Lancers sandwiching him in between them to prevent someone from getting a clear lock on him with a shoulder fired ground to air missile. He had a bodyguard in his car along with the pilot and the other cars were loaded with four Lancers each to provide him security.

When they landed at the space port, there was a small delegation waiting for him near a light freighter and the two shuttles from the attack. He was greeted at his car as he exited it by the Ambassador.

"Mister Connors, it is an honor to finally meet you Sir."

"Ambassador Penske, I'm not sure why meeting me is an honor but thank you. Now may I ask why you wanted this meeting today, here at the port?"

"Please, come with me." Penske motioned towards the freighter where Ezra could see several Fleet officers standing along with Greeson, Ponders and Susanne from the Settler's Office.

Penske introduced Ezra to the Fleet officer's which bothered him a bit since he recognized the Captain of the cruiser from his own days in the Fleet. The Captain's name was Overgaard and he stepped forward with a micro-disc in hand.

"Mister Connors, here is the authorization for you to take possession of this ship and the two shuttles. Since the Fleet has taken the vessels as prize vessels in the protection of Federation Citizen's and the risk you took to assist the Federation in removing the Rangers from our vocabulary, consider them as payment for Services Rendered."

"Captain Overgaard, from the damage to my home, I find it hard to believe that the Denali Rangers are finished."

64

"Mister Connors, with the capture of this ship, we also captured the last of the Denali leadership plus what we believe is a complete roster of the Rangers. Those not already known to be captured or dead are being ran down as we speak."

"Who authorized this transfer?"

"It comes from the Admiral of the Fleet along with no transfer taxes involved. Now the transfer is active today, but the ship and shuttles are to be taken to the Ship Yards on New Brumsfield where it will be upgraded as will the shuttles. This will also allow our people to insure there is nothing hidden behind a panel that can be useful to the Fleet."

Ezra accepted the micro-disc.

"Thank you Captain."

He looked up at the name painted on the side of the ship.

"Do me a favor Captain. Have the shipyard paint a new name on the ship."

"Certainly Sir. What name would you like on it?"

"Cherry Blossom"

Captain Overgaard gave him an odd look, then smiled.

"It will be taken care of Sir."

Ezra just nodded then walked over to Mister Penske from the Settler's Office.

"Mister Penske, would you be so kind as to insure the transfer of the ship is handled properly?"

Penske accepted the micro-disc then handed it to Susanne.

"Miss Wetherspoon will handle this transfer for the office, and insure it is properly taken care of."

"Mister Connors, if you can come with me, I'll have this processed and give you the paperwork and ship's title." Susanne spoke up.

65

"Certainly Miss Wetherspoon. Captain Overgaard, how many crew members are needed to fly this vessel?"

Ezra already knew the answer but was playing his part.

"Mister Connors, it can be handled with three crewmen counting the pilot."

Ezra stood for a moment thinking before answering.

"While at the shipyard, would you put the word out I need a crew for this vessel. I would prefer retired Fleet if possible and I'll pay the going rate. I'll provide quarters for them including spouses."

"I'll put the word out Mister Connors."

"Thank you Captain. Now Miss Wetherspoon, shall we go deal with the transfer of title?"

They took his aircar to the Settler's Office and they barely spoke to one another as she processed the title transfer. When she made the final entry and gave the command to process the title, she turned to Ezra while the process was taking place.

"Ezra, I heard about your friend Clare being wounded. I'm glad to hear she will recover from her wound."

"Thank you Susanne."

"Just so you do not misunderstand me, if you need someone to talk to, just give me a call. I don't mean someone to take to bed, just talk. In case Simon hasn't said anything, I'm seeing Lieutenant Holton, the Lancer Detachment Commander at the Embassy."

"Yes, I heard about that Susanne. From what I have heard, he is a good man. I hope things work out for the two of you."

"Thank You Ezra, and I hope your lady returns to you soon."

Ezra only smiled knowing Clare would never return.

When he returned to his home, Ezra sat at his computer for a long time as he searched his memory for a specific message drop address he was once given. When he recalled the address, he sent a message that he never expected to have to send.

"Karma has given me a profitable farm and income which is also because of the monetary gift you gave me. But the gift of the ship is calling attention to myself at higher levels of the Fleet and I only wish to disappear from the Fleet's memory. I understand the Lancers actions over the past months but once they are withdrawn, please forget who I am and where I am. Forget that I ever existed."

An hour later he received a reply to his message advising him that his wishes would be obeyed. Ezra could only laugh at the thought of Royalty bowing to his wishes.

Over the next six months, the Lancer Engineers were replaced by retired Engineers, then the Farm Lancers were replaced also by retired Lancers as word came down that the Denali Ranger were extinct. One factor that helped in the extinction of the Rangers was the death of Roger Denali in an accident in the iron mines.

With the addition of the retired Lancers came spouses and children. Ezra looked at the backgrounds of the spouses and put those to work in areas they once worked in before getting married. Two wives had been Lancer Medics, so Ezra had a small clinic built to deal with minor injuries on the Farm and Quarry.

A daycare and school were set up for the children with a large playground set up for use to help keep the children entertained when not in class.

Regina found two wives to help her around the main house so no one would be working long hours to maintain it and keep Ezra fed. His managers kept his businesses running smoothly but he was always moving around, not to keep an eye on them but to insure they had what was needed to keep things moving.

Fate Lends A Hand

With the return of the ship, the Cherry Blossom, Ezra started a small, sector freight business. He placed one shuttle at the Farm for his personal use, making moving around the planet faster than using aircars. He left the other shuttle at the space port to be leased by those who required such transportation, especially the Embassy and Settlers Office, who only had aircars for transportation.

He received a message from Clare nine months after she was wounded letting him know she was back to one hundred percent and had been retired from the Lancers on disability as the concern of another head injury would cause major problems. She told him that the time they had together was a wonderful memory but he needed someone that would not remind him of his past, and as much as she loved him, she was not that person. Clare advise him she had met a man outside of the Lancers who would make a good father for her children she hoped to produce and he understood the nightmares she still suffered, but were slowly weakening and going away.

Ezra returned her message with his hopes for her complete recovery and a wonderful life. He sat for a long time thinking how right she was even if the emotions between them seemed so right. He tucked the memories of her deep inside and returned his focus on his expanding business.

His haying business was slowing down so he began planting food crops to supplement the loss of hay income. One of his concerns was having employees with too little to do because once the crops were planted, they had a period of waiting before the next phase could be attended too.

The lumber business was stable with some shipments off planet to new frontier planets in the sector needing lumber until their own industry could be built. Ezra took further advantage of this situation on the planet Hildur. He took the Cherry Blossom to the planet and took a look at the possibility of opening business on the planet as the world was being opened to settlers.

Nearly thirty percent of Hildur was covered in forest. He carefully examined the Ecological report on the world then applied for title to ten thousand hectares of forest covered land. When the grant was authorized, he moved seven of his lumber crew who were single to the planet and set up a mill.

He chose the specific area carefully as there were hundreds of hectares of exotic woods which he knew he could sell at a premium on the open market.

One of the first things he did as the mill was being set up was to also build a nursery to grow seedlings for replanting, especially the more in demand exotic woods. His crew spent days gathering seedlings from the forests, transferring them to the nursery until needed.

Ezra underestimated the call for such exotics and within a year, he had broke even on the business even after hiring eight more men to harvest the timber and help in the mill. He also hired two of the men's wives to maintain the nurseries.

When it came time to replant a portion of the cleared ground, he hired teenagers from the nearest settlement for that project, paying them a decent wage based upon how many seedlings they could plant per day.

Five years after opening the Hildur operation, he was back on Nemea when he received an urgent call from his foreman on Hildur advising him that the tree harvester had fallen into an underground cavern as it moved from one tree to the next in an area which was sparsely grown.

Ezra asked if there were cranes on the planet which could lift the harvester out and was told that was being arranged but what was in the cavern was more important than the harvester. It appeared they had opened up a complex of tunnels, man-made tunnels.

He told them to remove the harvester, tarp over the opening, then stake it out while suspending all future harvesting until he got there. They were also to notify the Settlers Office

69

immediately of the situation and to just continue with the operation with the down timber. His transit time was one week and he would leave that day.

During transit he received another message that the crane operators advised them they could not get in close enough due to the unstable ground to lift the harvester out. The crane weighted three times what the harvester weighted.

Ezra checked the data on the harvester, did the math then placed a call to Fleet Sector Headquarters. The Assault Boats used by the Marines had a lift capacity greater than the weight of the harvester due to being used to move the Marine Engineers heavy equipment from ports to operational sites.

The Fleet authorized the use of Assault Boats to remove the harvester due to the discovery of the cavern/tunnels and a Marine Assault Carrier was six days out from Hildur.

They landed at the Kankakee Space Port at the capital of Kankakee with Isaac, Ezra's logging chief, and Arron, the harvester operator waiting for him at the bottom of the ramp. Before Ezra could say anything, Arron spoke up.

"Mister Connors, I'm real sorry about the harvester. I tried to save it, but it happened so fast I barely made it out before she was underground."

Ezra stepped to Arron, placed his hand on his shoulder and smiled.

"Son, are you hurt?"

"Just a sprained wrist from landing wrong Sir."

"Are you still on my payroll?"

"Yes Sir."

"Then why don't we forget about what happened and why it happened for now, and focus on getting the harvester out of that hole and back to work. You couldn't have known the ground was going to open up and try to swallow you, so forget about it. I'm

70

just glad you were not seriously injured. Be hard to find a good operator out here on the frontier."

"Thanks Mister Connors."

"Now Isaac, what can you tell me about the condition of the harvester?"

"Not much. The air coming out of that hole is pretty foul. The short time I was able to look down it seemed the arm is out of kilter, and there was hydraulic fluid all over the beam. I suspect since Arron was reaching for a tree when the bottom went, the arm was torqued as it dropped, over-pressuring the system and blowing a few lines. We won't know much of anything until we get it back above ground and completely go through it."

Ezra thoughtfully nodded then looked back up the ramp to see the ship's cargo chief standing at the top.

"Chief, I need three rebreathers and high density lights."

The Chief gave him a thumbs up and disappeared into the hold of the ship.

"Arron, go help the Chief."

When they arrived at the work site, Ezra had Isaac take him over the actual sight so he could get a bird's eye view of the situation.

"Boss, I know you told me to cover the hole, but the air was so foul, I decided to leave it open, maybe clear the air some but up here, even with the fans blowing down, you can still smell the stench."

"Isaac, you were here on the scene, not me. You made the right decision. Never second guess the man on the scene if you are ten parsecs away. Now set us down and we'll see what we can do about tackling this problem."

Once on the ground, Ezra walked the ground up to the first of the fallen trees. He looked at the situation then turned to Isaac.

"Get everyone out here, bring the haulers up to the point where the ground begins to feel shaky. I want the area around the hole cleared out for one hundred meters all around it."

"Isaac, as the crews are getting things lined out, go back into town and buy thirty millimeter steel cable, clamps, hooks, and chains. Once the timber is ready, we tie onto them and drag them out, then keep clearing until we are at the point we have the area cleared out. Understand what I want?"

"Yeah boss, drag lines. I'll get right on it."

As the rest of the crew were gathering their equipment, Ezra had Arron put on a rebreather then grabbed another man to do the same before outfitting himself. He was going to take Arron into the hole and examine the harvester with the other man staying on top as a look-out in case they needed help.

The cutting arm of the harvester was barely below the surface and they were able to skinny down it to the cab. They had to be careful as hydraulic fluid covered a lot of the metal surfaces making it slick. Ezra flashed his light around the inside of the hole and felt his stomach knot up.

Ezra saw what would be considered walls with strange, alien markings on them, then two doors further down the cavern or tunnel which he was not sure which they were in. He took a small video camera from his jacket pocket and made a slow sweep with it twice before signaling Arron to go back up and out of the hole. He slipped once on the cutting arm, but was able to hang on, then get his footing back before he was able to crawl out of the hole.

As they were walking back to the staging area where his crews were gathering he thought to himself that Karma or Fate had once more placed him in a position he had no desire to be. He had no choice but to report what he had found to the authorities.

At the staging area, when he removed the rebreather, the stench of the hole seemed to have clung to his clothing. He couldn't send his men into that area without rebreathers. He contacted Isaac and told him to buy as many rebreathers as he could lay his hands on for the workers.

He gave his rebreather to one of the timber crew and told Arron to get busy with what they had until Isaac returned with more equipment. By the time Isaac returned, they had four trees ready to be drug out, and were working on a fifth. Isaac took over supervision of the task, assigning men to specific tasks, then making sure everyone understood safety came before anything else.

Three men to a trimming and chaining crew where two would trim the limbs from the tree while the third watched to insure they were safe. They would rotate as they moved from tree to tree to give each man a period of rest before moving on to the next tree.

Once the tree was ready, a chain crew came in, wrapped the tree trunk with a chain then drug a long cable in, hooked it to the wrapped chain so one of the heavy lift machines from the saw mill could drag it out, then place it on a carrier for transport to the mill.

Ezra realized they had brought out all of the heavy lift tractors out to the site which meant there were no tractors at the saw mill to unload the trailers hauling the logs away. He sent one back with the instructions to only off load the trailers as they came in staging the logs until they could later process them.

But it didn't take long to realize they still had to clear the removed limbs from the site, so they changed tactics and drug the entire tree out, then removed the limbs. Soon they had all of the downed trees cleared away and the crews went to work of those still standing.

Once everything was lined out and going as well as it could under the circumstance, Ezra took the aircar into Kankakee to report what he had found to the Settlers Office. The Protocol Officer at the Settlers Office was a new man, one that Ezra had not met before. He was young and stuffy as Ezra tried to explain what he had found.

Ezra downloaded a copy of the video to the office computer for him to review which Ezra was then told it had to go to Sector Headquarters before he could do anything. Ezra thanked him then went to his ship, loaded the video into the ships computer and sent it to Fleet Headquarters along with a copy to the blind address he had only used once before, along with a written report including his evaluation of the Settlers Officer Protocol Officer. He did not wait for a reply as he returned to the work site.

When Ezra called a stop for the day, instead of going to the small cabin he had near the mill, he returned to the ship to see what replies may have came in to his message to the Fleet. He had several awaiting him.

The first or oldest message came from the Sector Headquarters of the Settlers Authority ordering him to stop all clearing operations and to make no attempt to retrieve the harvester until the proper authorities could arrive on the scene to evaluate the situation.

The next message was time stamped within an hour of him sending his message to the Fleet and it was from the blind address acknowledging receipt of his message.

The third message was from Sector Fleet Headquarters approving his operations with a warning to be cautious not to create any more damage to the site as necessary in the removal of the harvester. It also instructed all Fleet units responding to this situation to coordinate with him and that the Connors Lumber Company – Hildur, would supply under contract any and all materials to shore up the site to prevent further cave-ins at the standard Fleet purchase price for such materials. He was also authorized an additional fifteen percent above material costs for labor and transportation. Any additional costs would have to be negotiated at the time required.

Ezra just smiled knowing that the Fleet had been told how to handle the situation and it put him basically in the driver's seat.

The last message was from a Doctor E. Lee stating they would arrive in five days from New Brumsfield to take over the site for exploration and research. Again a word of caution concerning the further destruction of the cavern/tunnel and any artifacts that might be present at the time of the removal of the harvester.

The last trees were being removed when the Marine's Assault Boat landed in the staging area. Senior Lieutenant Horner and Gunnery Sergeant Farnsworth of the Engineers went directly to the site after meeting Ezra.

Ezra remembering the problems getting into the hole had ladders made from wood so that there was no metal to cause a spark in case part of the stench were Petro-carbons in the air. The Marines brought better equipment to test air quality and determined it was not a bio-hazard or had any flammable content. It just smelled bad from inside the cavern.

The Marines were in the hole for nearly an hour examining the harvester for how to best raise it from the hole, then the ceiling of the cavern around the harvester to determine how to shore it up prior to lifting the harvester out.

As the Gunny contacted the Marine Carrier in orbit with the list of personnel and equipment to bring to the surface, the Lieutenant got with Ezra and Isaac about the timbers needed to shore up the cavern ceiling before they tried to lift the harvester out. Isaac took the list and headed for the mill to find the timbers needed, or to have specific timbers milled.

Ezra's crew assisted the Marines in getting the cavern ceiling shored up then stood aside as the Marines rigged the harvester for lifting. A ladder was placed down on the harvester and the Gunny moved into position so when the Assault Boat centered on the harvester, he could hook the chain lead to the cabled hook under the boat. As soon as he had the chains secured, he scrambled up the ladder, pulled it out of the way then moved away from the hole.

The lift went better than they planned with only dirt falling into the hole from around its edge as the harvester cleared the rim. The harvester was sat down behind the staging area with Arron waiting until the Marines cleared the chains to climb into the cab and started the fusion engine. He ran a diagnostic of the harvester then shut everything down after printing out the checklist.

Ezra looked at the checklist then told Arron to get the harvester repaired so they could check out the cutting head. He then went to look at the hole as Marines scrambled down the ladders to check the timbers and determine any additional shoring that might be necessary.

When Lieutenant Horner came back to the surface, he gave Ezra a material list for additional timbers. Ezra suggest they also build a stairway down to the cavern floor to make life easier for anyone going in and out of the hole. Horner approved the idea and Ezra turned that project over to Isaac to complete.

The Marines then brought blowers in with long stretches of flexible duct to exchange the air in the cavern as well as possible. It helped, but the stench seemed to come from further into the tunnel, and the Marines were not authorized to venture further into the tunnel until the scientists arrived.

The next two days were taken up with just insuring that the ground was stable, and the air exchange was continued. Ezra stayed out of the way as much as possible, often just sitting in his aircar, watching the interaction between his men and the Marines.

Ezra read a story from the Interplanetary News Service about the activity on Hildur and the mysterious hole discovered there. There was a photo of him in the article, but he was thankful it was more current than others possibly out there with his heavy beard and long hair.

Once more Fate has brought him into the public eye.

Earthly Troubles

Ezra, Isaac, and Lieutenant Horner stood watching the shuttle land containing the scientific team that were to investigate the cavern. Horner had advised Ezra that he considered Ezra the main point of contact with the scientists until the Fleet said otherwise. Horner said he was only there to provide the muscle the team might need in their investigation.

As the ramp was coming down on the shuttle, Ezra moved towards it, stopping back from it to greet the team, especially the team leader, one Doctor Lee.

The first people off the shuttle were carrying cases and Ezra asked about Doctor Lee and was told still on the shuttle. He waited for a minute or two, then a single individual came off the shuttle that was either lost, or was Doctor Lee.

If this was Doctor Lee, then he was a she. She was of Asian decent with long, coal black hair was below her shoulders and wisping in the light breeze. She was dressed in a form fitting jumpsuit which showed she had a modest figure. Her heart shaped face with her dark eyes and modest lips looked as if she belonged in a vid show, not digging in dirt.

He greeted her as she started to walk past him.

"Doctor Lee?"

"Yes, who are you?"

"Ezra Connors at your service Doctor Lee."

He offered his hand which she looked at then accepted it. Her hand was small but had strength to it in the short time she allowed the physical contact. Ezra stood one point nine meters and she would not even come up to his shoulders.

She looked over at the cleared site then back at him.

"I understood the Settlers Authority told you not to disturb anything."

"True Doctor, but the Fleet authorized the removal of my harvester and the clearing of the ground in order to insure your safe examination of the cavern. In fact, you messaged me advising me to be careful not to disturb the site any more than possible. We have been very careful not to create any more problems in the cavern than needed to insure you and your teams safety."

She gave him a blank look, tilted her head to the right then responded.

"Oh, yes, I did, didn't I. What is the situation with the foul air that was reported."

"The Marines have been pumping fresh air into the cavern for several days now. There is still a stench but not as bad as it earlier was. You can work in the area without a rebreather, but to be honest, it might still be a good idea to use them."

"Alright then Mister Connors. I'm here now so you can go back to whatever business you have here on Hildur."

She turned away and started to walk off from him. He reached out and took her arm, stopping her from leaving.

"Doctor Lee, this is my land, my business and the Fleet has placed me as point of contact for this situation. I may not know anything about your business, but this is my business. I will not be dismissed like some underling."

She looked down at his hand on her arm then tried to pull out of his grip, but found it impossible to accomplish.

"Let go of me sir."

"Doctor, I'm the person that reported this when someone else may have just recovered the equipment, then filled the hole in to prevent his business from being shut down. I'm in on this whether you like it or not."

Lee looked over at Horner who was standing near with a neutral look on his face then back up at Ezra.

"Alright Mister Connors, but please try to stay out of the way."

"You mean out of your way? No problem Doctor Lee."

He released her allowing her to walk away. Horner stepped closer as they both watched her walk towards the hole in the ground.

"Mister Connors, is it me or is she where she doesn't want to be?"

"Yeah, did you notice the look on her face as she came off the shuttle? I think she is out of her league and she is scared, yet will not admit it to herself."

"I've seen that look before Mister Connors, during a drop into a hot drop zone. Why do I think you've had the same experience?"

Ezra never responded to Horner's comment, as he walked away towards the hole to be near if needed. He stopped short and turned to Horner who had followed him.

"Lieutenant, request the file on Lee. I have a feeling this is her first dance and if so, we need to take extra measures to insure her and her team are safe as they explore the underground."

"Will do Mister Connors."

Ezra moved closer and watched as the scientists broke out protective gear, got rigged up, then opened cases with several different types of instruments before heading down into the cavern. He focused on Lee as much as possible and caught the distinct quiver in her hands as she reached for a high intensity light. When she paused for a second at the top of the stairs, Ezra could only smile at himself seeing she was in fact scared to go down into the cavern.

"You going down in the hole boss?"

Ezra didn't turn to look at Isaac standing beside him as he wanted to watch Doctor Lee move down the stairway.

"Yeah, I think I'd better."

"Then you're going to need this."

Ezra looked over at Isaac to see him holding his rebreather out to him.

"Thanks Isaac. How's the repairs on the harvester going?"

"Looks good boss. With luck we'll make a test run with it this afternoon. If we have a go, what do you what us to do?"

"Cut more timber that we can make into shoring timbers if needed. Have the mill go ahead and cut them up into standard sizes, and if we do not need them, we can always go back and cut boards from them. We will lose a bit of material that way, but I'll either find a way to write it off, or just take the hit. Either way, we stay ahead of the game here at the cavern."

"Alright boss, I'll let Arron know. Now be careful down there."

"Always Isaac."

When he went down into the cavern, Ezra found Lee sitting on a three-legged stool reading from her pad as one of her male team members was standing beside her holding a piece of the ceiling material. He moved close enough to hear what she was saying to him.

"Jonathon, there is nothing in the planetary survey to indicate there was a cavern in this region. Nothing at all."

Ezra stepped closer.

"Doctor Lee."

She jumped off her stool from him speaking to her from behind.

"What!"

"Doctor Lee, the Marines made a low level pass at fifty meters and the sensors on their Assault Boats never registered

80

anything except the hole itself. It seems that the material covering the ceiling and walls absorb the sensors output."

"Oh, okay, thank you. Jonathon, we need to get samples into the lab to find out what we are dealing with in here."

"Doctor Lee," Ezra once more spoke up. "The Fleet has several samples already and they are enroute to Zyra for testing. Each sample was inspected to ensure there were no markings or graphics on them."

She looked at him for a moment before speaking.

"Jonathon, go ahead and run the tests, then we can compare them to what the Fleet discovers. Mister Connors, is there anything else I need to know?"

"Not that I can think of at the moment Doctor."

She just nodded and sat back down on her stool and returned to reading the planetary report as her team members were taking samples of all manner of things plus photographs of the markings on the walls and ceilings.

Ezra moved out of the way and found a place he could watch everyone as they worked. Lieutenant Horner came down with a pad in hand and located Ezra. He just walked up to Ezra and handed him the pad. On the pads screen was the Federation Intelligence Report of Doctor Emily Natalya Lee.

Doctor Lee, age thirty-six, was born in the city of Taegu on the Korean Peninsula of the East China Prefect on Earth. Her education started at the University at Seoul, then she received her Doctorate on Zyra in Xeno-Anthropology. It was noted in her background her father was killed in a cave-in of an underground mushroom farm he operated caused by an earthquake. She was trapped under the mushroom growth tables for two days before being rescued.

Ezra now understood why she was scared. She was borderline claustrophobic, which made him wonder how she could travel across space enclosed in a steel box. He was focused on reading her file when a loud, booming voice echoed through the cavern.

"FREEZE!

Ezra immediately recognized it came from the external speakers on a battle helmet. He looked up to see a Marine quickly moving towards the doors at the side of the cavern, then one of the scientists standing at the door, looking around in terror.

"Shit." Ezra thought as he also began moving towards the door. The Marine got there first.

"What the hell do you think you are doing mister?"

The Marine was a Corporal and was not concerned about anyone's title at the moment. The man at the door stuttered out a reply.

"I…I was going to see what is behind this door."

"Mister, we haven't opened those doors because we do not know what is behind them, and we were waiting for you scientists to tell us to get them open. You never know what is on the other side of a door that might just kill you. Now step aside, and when Doctor Lee tells us, we will open the doors with you folks above ground. Am I clear on this?"

The man looked as if he was about to panic when Ezra walked up beside him.

"Sir, the Corporal is only trying to ensure your safety, so please move away from the door until it is determined that they need to be opened. Marines are skilled at opening doors when something on the other side might harm them."

"Yeah, okay, sorry."

The man moved away, looked around then went to Lee who was standing, watching the event from her position in the sunlight. Ezra turned to the Marine.

"Corporal, post a man at both doors so this will not happen again."

"Yes Sir, Mister Connors."

Ezra then walked over to Lee who was talking to the man who had started to open the door. He heard her tell him it was alright, she should have considered that the doors had not been opened and checked for danger. She looked at Ezra, then dismissed the man to find something else to do before turning to Ezra.

"Thank you Mister Connors for smoothing that out. I should have talked with the Marines before assigning tasks. Again, is there anything else I need to know?"

"Doctor Lee, I'm sure something will come up that either myself or Lieutenant Horner will have to deal with for you. One or both of us will always be down here when you and your team are exploring the cavern. Do not hesitate to come to us for assistance."

He turned and walked away from her before she could respond. When he finally turned back to her, she was once again sitting on her stool, reading whatever it was on her pad.

He had been around people in her field before and they were always moving about, getting into things, overseeing their peoples work, but she was sitting there, in the sunlight, not moving. Yes, she was scared and trying not to show it.

It was over an hour later that he watched her get up and walk over to Horner who was across the cavern from him. She talked to Horner for a minute then started up the stairs. Horner came up on his speakers.

"Marines on me. Everyone else clear the cavern."

The civilians began gathering up their equipment as the Marines in the cavern moved to gather around Horner. Ezra moved to Horner to listen to his instructions.

"Men, we've talked about this before so I'm going to keep it short. You know your teams, so each team take a door and examine it carefully before any attempt is made to open it. No one, and I mean no one is to open a door without talking to me first. Clear?"

Everyone acknowledged his orders, then moved towards the doors, gathering into teams as they moved. Ezra moved closer to Horner.

"How long do you think it'll be before you open them up?"

"Mister Connors, all things considered, how about some time in the next century?"

Ezra chuckled.

"Yeah, I know the feeling. Do me a favor, do not open them until I come back down. I'm going to change into something more applicable for the job."

Horner gave Ezra a sideways look then nodded his understanding. Ezra just patted Horner on the shoulder, then went up the stairs. He never spoke to anyone above ground as he went to his aircar, then flew to his cabin to change. In the cabin was the bag he had been given years before with his Lancer uniform and gear.

Ezra changed as quickly as he could ensuring the armor was in place in their leg and arm pouches. He had gained a few pounds but everything still fit except for his helmet. Once he had his hair pulled back, the helmet adjusted to his head, but there was no way for it to seal with the face shield down due to his beard so he decided to only use the visor, which would still give him the information and sight he would need in a dark environment.

He added a small respirator for his nose and mouth, hooking it into the helmets small air reserve in case of need. When he powered up the AI, he saw he still had plenty of power for today's mission, but he would need to charge it as soon as possible.

Body armor, equipment vest, blades, pistol, and carbine were checked twice before he left the cabin. As long as it had been since he wore this uniform, it felt natural to him. When he landed at the site, everyone noticed how he was dressed with his respirator unfastened from one side of his helmet. He instructed his helmet's AI to locate the Marines frequency and lock it in during this operation.

"Lieutenant Horner, this is Connors, how do you read me, over?"

"Connors, this is Horner, loud and clear, over."

"Status over?"

"Just waiting for you, over."

"Be there in a minute, out."

Ezra had set the aircar down in his normal place, stepped out of the car and snapped his carbine into place across his chest, as he walked towards the cavern and the stairs to the bottom. The civilians just looked at him oddly, but the Marines above the ground moved out of his way, giving him a wide path to walk. One of Ezra's workers noticed how the Marines were watching Ezra and quietly asked what was going on.

"Mister, that is a Lancer uniform. You can buy the pants and jacket in just about any Second Hand Store in the Federation, but no one can get their hands on the armor, equipment vest and weapons in such a manner, but that helmet says it all."

"What's the big deal about the helmet?"

"See that Crimson Dragon on the helmet? That's the Second Battalion, Seventh Lancer Regiment. They don't come any tougher than those boys and girls. Legend is they have never given a single meter to the enemy. If they take a step forward, they'll not take a step back. They'll die in place first. That boss of yours is not someone to screw with."

"Really? Man you have to be wrong, Mister Connors is one of the nicest men it has been my pleasure to work for."

"Yeah, he is a very nice gentleman, but we've yet to see him pissed off."

Ezra never heard a word being spoken about him as he went down the stairs. He was just tired and unknown to the rest of the universe, very pissed off. No matter what he tried to do, Karma kept throwing him back into the public eye and he was tired of hiding. He walked over to Horner and asked his plan.

"Mister Connors, we're taking the left door first. The piston ram will open the door, two Chem-flares will be tossed in, then Corporal Knipplemeir will enter ahead of his team. Once that room is secure, the other team will repeat the process on their door."

"Lieutenant, I'm taking the door on the left. You take the one on the right once I call clear. Be ready to support Knipplemeir's team if it drops in the pot. Any questions?"

"Yeah, one. Is that your uniform or did you buy it at a resale shop?"

"It's all mine Lieutenant."

Horner reached down and grabbed Ezra's wrist. Just above the cuff were the outlines of two small stripes or bars with three stars above them. Each bar stood for a battle wound serious enough to require a hospital stay. The stars were for valor, usually earned with the battle wounds, and they were not awarded to everyone. Ezra had removed them from his uniform jacket, but the outlines remained.

"Mister Connors, you led, we'll follow all the way into Hades if that is where you are heading."

"We're all headed in that direction, I just hope today is not that day. Let's do this."

As Ezra moved towards the left door, Horner called out instructions.

"Corporal Knipplemeir, Mister Connors has your team, follow his orders. I have the team on the right. Let's do this people. Heads up, stay sharp!"

Ezra moved to the left side of the door and reached out for the Chem-flare the man behind him was holding. He looked across the door at Corporal Knipplemeir who held the other flare. He held the flare up to indicate to Knipplemeir to get ready then activated his as Knipplemeir copied him. Once both flares were bright, Ezra yelled 'blow it', and pressed himself against the wall. The door silently blew open, then as it was still swinging open, Ezra tossed his flare in then watched as Knipplemeir tossed his in. With his right hand he grabbed the pistol grip of his carbine while with his left he held up his open hand and counted down five seconds with his fingers then turned into the door ready for a fight with Knipplemeir following in behind him.

He sweep half the room twice before calling clear. Ezra heard Knipplemeir call the same, then he called on the radio to take the next door. He just stood in what looked to him to be living quarters but none of the furniture looked like it was made for humans. And the stench in the room was strong enough to penetrate his respirator.

"Corporal Knipplemeir, get that door off it's hinges and keep this room lit until we can get some light sets down here."

"Yes Sir. Peters, get the door off the hinges. Samuels, watch the flares and keep this room lit up. Everyone watch for hidden access panels in here. Stay alert!"

Ezra smiled under his respirator at Knipplemeir thinking about the possibility of secret panels in the room. As he exited the room, he met Horner coming out of the other room. Horner described the other room exactly like the room Ezra had taken. Ezra told Horner what he had ordered Knipplemeir to do. Horner turned back to his team and gave the same orders.

As Ezra moved towards the stairs, he heard Horner come up on the radio to his Gunny, ordering ventilation and lights brought down. Ezra turned back away from the stairs and looked into the abyss of the tunnel still to be explored. The Marines had set movement detectors about fifty meters into the darkness, but it was still needed to be lighted and explored.

He walked out into the sunlight and just stood for a moment to let the adrenalin ease out of his body before moving on to his next thoughts or actions. Ezra saw Isaac standing by the Gunny and walked over to him.

"Isaac, pull everyone out but one man to act as liaison between the Marines, Scientists and yourself. Make sure he has good communications and understands if they ask for it, he goes through you to arrange for it without pause. Got it?"

"Got it boss. What about you?"

Ezra raised his visor up and just looked at Isaac then turned to the Gunny.

"Gunny, you just make sure that whomever Isaac posts here is in the loop at all times, understand?"

"Understand Mister Connors."

Ezra walked over to his aircar, climbed in, then flew back to his cabin. When he landed at the cabin he just sat in the aircar as his hands began to shake. He closed his eyes and let his mind chide him for what he had done.

"You stupid bastard, what were you thinking? No, you weren't thinking, you were reacting, but to what? Were you trying to impress the lady doctor? Were you trying to impress the Marines and your crew? Bullshit, they already respect you, but let's face the truth, you were hoping that entering that room would end it all for you. It looks like Karma has done bit you in the ass in a major way. It's not your fault you survived when your crew was lost. Stop running from that reality, because it looks as if the Fates will not allow that to happen."

He had no idea how long he sat thinking about what he had done, thinking about the past, and could not envision the future. He sat until his helmet's AI alerted him that he only had twenty-percent power left in the helmet. It was then he realized he had to have been sitting in the aircar for nearly three hours.

Going into the cabin he plugged the helmet into a power outlet. Once at one hundred percent, the helmet would be good for another six months of hard use or five years of just sitting in his bags.

His cabin was basically one large room with everything out in the open, then an enclosed sanitary facility with a real shower in it at the back of the cabin. He laid everything on the kitchen table for now as he stripped for the shower.

Ezra stood under the hot water from the shower a long time as if the hot water would wash his sins away, but there was not enough water in the universe to do that very thing. He decided he would have his hair cut and beard trimmed to Lancer standards so he could properly wear his helmet if needed again. And thinking about that long tunnel of darkness in the cavern, he would need it again. He had started down a path he could not turn away from now.

He stepped out of the shower, grabbed a towel and began drying his head and hair as he walked into the living part of the cabin. He heard a noise, looked out from under the towel and there stood Doctor Lee in the doorway, her eyes wide and her mouth open in surprise.

"Oh God!"

She uttered as she turned back through the door and closed it behind her. Ezra looked down at himself, nude and dripping water all over the floor and could only chuckle at the incident. He quickly dried off, put on a pair of trousers and a pull over shirt, then went to the door barefooted to see if she was still present.

Lee was standing beside on of the porch pillars, looking like she was holding it up. Ezra opened the door and stepped out onto the porch.

"Doctor Lee, do you need to see me?"

After he said see me, he held back a laugh since she had most certainly saw him.

"Excuse me Doctor, I meant talk to me."

Lee turned around, her olive complexion dark from the blush she was experiencing.

"Yes Mister Connors I do. I am really sorry, but I was told this was your office, not your home. I would have knocked instead of just walking in on you that way."

"Doctor Lee, this is my home away from home which is on Nemea. Besides, we are both adults, so let us just forgot what happened and take care of business. What do you need to see me about?"

"Thank you. First of all my team will spend the night on our transport then in the morning, our temporary shelters will be brought down so we can stay planet side during our research. I talked to your man, Isaac about borrowing a half-dozen men to assist in setting the shelters up which he told me that would not be a problem."

"Isaac was correct. We have a contract with the Fleet to provide such assistance when necessary. So what are your concerns?"

"Sheltered working space. After talking with my team, we need a much larger space then we can bring down to examine what is brought out of the cavern. Isaac said that had to be cleared through you."

"You're talking about a more permanent structure then?"

"Yes, someplace where we can spread out plus hold our equipment."

"Doctor Lee, if you can provide the dimensions for such a facility, it will be built. I can bring in specific contractors to deal with what my men cannot achieve, and don't concern yourself with costs, as I'm fairly certain once you get well into this project, your budget will be increased to cover those costs."

"Thank you Mister Connors, I'll get with my team this evening and get the requirements worked out."

She offered her hand to him which he accepted.

"Doctor Lee, you're welcome, and please, call me Ezra."

She smiled.

"Then please call me Emily."

She released his hand and stepped off the porch for her aircar. Ezra could still feel the heat from her soft hand yet there was strength in that hand. He had not been with a woman in nearly two solar years and this one interested him.

He could not have imagined what Emily was thinking as she returned to her chauffeured aircar. She looked back at him as she took her seat in the car thinking she had not been with a man since her engagement to another Doctor had ended nearly three years ago.

She could remember nearly every scar on his body from that brief moment of viewing him naked, dripping water from the shower. Her file on Ezra Connors said he was the richest man in the sector and had become so through hard work and clarity of thought in his investments, but his calloused hands and firm body said he did not just allow others to handle the work. Then there was the uniform and weapons. This was not noted in his file so there was something in his background that intrigued her.

"Yes, he thought, let her get settled in then maybe invite her to dinner. Get to know her better and see where it might take them."

He returned to his bathroom and began removing the bulk of his beard. He was not going to totally expose himself, but he was going to make it more business-like, then tomorrow he would go into Kankakee and get his hair cut if time allowed.

"Remember, he told himself, you are not looking for a playmate or even a spouse, just someone for polite, intelligent conversation. Yeah, and that olive skin on white sheets would also be nice."

Stages

Once Ezra had the specifications in hand for the research facility as Lee referred to the building, he went into Kankakee to arrange for contractors to fulfill the work requirements his own men could not deal with. There was no debate on costs as he told the contractors to get out to the site and get to work as the scientists needed the facility to progress with their work.

His own saw mill was working extras hours to produce the lumber needed to replace the air dried lumber being used to build the facility as they still had orders for lumber away from the cavern exploration.

One thing that Ezra saw that was missed by Lee and her team, was what to do with the items brought up from the cavern once they had been examined and tested. Without prompting by others, he had a second building constructed as a warehouse.

He also had the ground tested, shored up better in the cavern and a road laid between the cavern and buildings so the transportation of items would not be over soft ground, especially since the rainy season was just over a month away.

Isaac mentioned that the open hole in the ground plus the way the terrain lay meant that water run-off would find its way into the cavern, so they needed pumps to keep it pumped out. Relying on his youth as a farmer, Ezra had the ground terraced so the majority of the run-off would be diverted away from the hole, plus he had a light framework built over it, then plastron canvas stretched over that to keep the rain out.

Ezra sat in his office/home and looked at the bills stacking up as he authorized payment for each item. If he could get sixty percent back, he would break even for the year at the rate of sales so far, and maybe still make a profit if lucky. He had the money, but it was his business instinct that kept getting in the way of progress.

The first items had been brought up and were being examined in the research facility while the Marines had slowly moved down the tunnel, fixing lighting to the ceiling as they opened more doors to discover what were behind them. It was finally discovered that the stench came from the sites waste transfer system which was clogged and rotting. The problem with clearing that system was that the scientists wanted samples of the waste for lab testing.

Seeing Ezra in battle gear working with the Marines became a common sight and no one ignored his instructions. An Infantry section was dropped to support the opening of the tunnels and rooms leaving the Engineers to safely crack the doors, and insure the areas they were clearing were structurally safe for the scientists.

Ezra was not the only person to notice that when Doctor Lee was in the cavern, she stayed close to the hole, the opening above the cavern. The first thought was she was scared of the darkness within but once well lighted, it became obvious she was afraid of being underground, in an enclosed space.

But what little contact he had with her had become pleasant as even her tone had lightened as she spoke. She seemed comfortable around him unlike when she first met him at the shuttle. They often talked business over lunch if the situation presented itself, but she was always business-like and most contact came from her passing him a note on something she needed done.

It was a month after she had blundered in on him coming out of the shower that he asked her to dinner. The Marines had put up a temporary Mess Facility to support them on the ground and Ezra felt it was best to utilize that location instead of his cabin with the bed out in the open. He didn't want her to think that was all he had on his mind. One thing he knew from experience, was that regardless how appealing a woman, how they reacted in bed could be disappointing.

Dinner was simple mess fare of pasta with a meat sauce and diced sausage. A white wine was allowable for those off duty and would not be assuming duty until the next morning and even then it was rationed.

Ezra and Emily talked about how the project was going, if there were any additional needs he could take care of, and how her folks were getting along with the Marines and his own people. He had hired an additional ten men whose function was to assist the scientists in moving items from the cavern topside and into the research facility. This allowed him to put his timber crews back to work and only came to the site if additional shoring was required.

As the meal was winding down, he finally dropped a bomb on her as she was taking a bite of pasta, nearly causing her to choke on it.

"Emily, I have been wondering. How do you deal with transiting from one planet to another being claustrophobic?"

She gagged on the pasta, the coughed it back onto her plate.

"What makes you think I'm claustrophobic?"

"Your actions since you have been here and the fact you were once trapped underground by a cave-in caused by an earthquake as a child."

She leaned back in her chair, then took a swallow of wine before answering.

"The only way you would know that information about me was if you had access to my Federation Intelligence File for my security clearance. I find that interesting since the file on you seems to be one written by a mystery writer."

Ezra laughed.

"So, you did a bit of checking up on me too. I guess I can understand that considering our first meeting."

"Yes, but that was not the only reason. I've watched how you deal with your people and the Marines. I noticed how you carried yourself, as if you were used to being in command. Not arrogant like some rich men carry themselves. Yes, I know about your wealth and how you came by it. I thought it was odd that you came from nowhere to become one of the richest, and maybe soon the richest man in this quadrant. But your start-up capital seems to have came out of thin air. Nothing in your bio suggests you striking it rich or being born wealthy. You interest me Ezra Connors, if that is actually your real name. But let us, you and me have an understanding. If you wish me in your bed, it will be after I know the truth of who you really are. Not before. There is no doubt you were a Lancer, but unless you are a skinned Centaurian, you have another life before becoming a Lancer. And your accent suggests you are not a Centaurian."

Ezra just looked at her with a slight grin on his face. She had just told him the reward he would receive if she knew the truth about him, yet was she worth it? But sex was just that, sex. And as the old saying goes, there is no such thing as bad sex, just some is better than others. But in a manner she just became a prostitute with her payment being his life story. Again, was she worth it? Then the comment about his accent. One never hears how they sound when they talk, all they hear is the echo, but never the actual tone and accent.

"Skinned is not the polite word for a denuded Centaurian. But what of my accent? I've been out in the universe for several decades, do I have an accent giving away my place of birth?"

"Not completely Ezra, but yes, you do have one which to my ear, sounds like a North American accent from Earth. It crops up when you are in a hurry or stressed such as when down in the tunnel working with the Marines and time is short."

Again he just looked at her for a moment.

"So I tell you my life story, the one you suspect I am hiding, and you jump in my bed?"

"Ezra, we both know what we want. I knew the moment I saw you standing in your office, naked as a newborn, I wanted you. I've seen you looking at me when you had better things to do and I have no doubt if this subject had not came up, that if I got up to refresh my tea, you'd be watching my hip movements as I walked away from the table. Lie to me and tell me otherwise."

"No Emily, I will not lie to you."

"Then let us finish our dinner, then you can walk me to my quarters, and you can kiss me goodnight. But that is as good as it gets until my conditions are met."

"And if I cannot meet your conditions?"

"Then we shall go through the rest of our lives knowing that we missed out on what could have been a very pleasant relationship away from work."

She just looked at him waiting for his response. When he remained quiet, she broke the silence.

"Now as far as my being claustrophobic, I view the ships I travel in as a sturdy house unaffected by earthquakes and incapable of trapping me under tons of dirt and rock. It is the mental inability for me to come to grips with the smell of dirt or even knowing its there that alludes me."

Ezra took a drink of wine.

"We'll have to work on your fears, but what if I lie to you to get you into my bed?"

"Then you had better pray I never find out because I will serve your testicles to you on a bed of rice."

"Fair enough. More wine?"

The rest of dinner was fairly quiet after that. They walked separated from each other to her quarters where she opened her door then stood in the doorway, bringing her to his height. The kiss was long, slow as he kept his hands properly place on her body. When they broke the kiss, she gently rubbed his beard.

"I guess I can get use to this." She then turned into her quarters and waited until he stepped back before shutting the door.

Ezra looked at the closed door several moments before smiling and walked towards his aircar. He wasn't ready yet to expose himself even just to her, but so far, it felt as if doing so would be worth the problems that might arise from doing so. Ezra decided to let this go as is for a time to see how things evolve.

Two days later Ezra stood in the cavern watching Emily as she stood looking down the tunnel knowing she had to go down it to see what a crew had found but it seemed her legs would not work for her. He walked over to her, reached down and took her hand. To most people it seemed she had a blank look on her face, but to Ezra beneath her expression was one of fear.

"One step at a time Emily. Just take it one step at a time."

He took a step holding her hand and she stepped with him. They walked nearly half the distance she needed to go when he stopped and pried her hand from his, then stepped away from her.

"Emily, I would never place you at risk as I have too much to gain with you, so if you wish to know about me, learn about yourself. Look at the people around you moving in and out of this area as if they were above ground, or on a ship in transit. If you want me, then put aside the irrational fear coursing through your body and mind right now, and rejoin the human race."

He leaned over, kissed her on the cheek, then walked away, back towards the opening, never looking back at her. When he entered the open area he turned back to see she was gone. He smiled to himself and left the cavern knowing she had to deal with her fears as he had to deal with his own.

Emily stood in the small quarters looking at what appeared to be a computer, yet there was no keyboard, power cables, or anything that resembled even the most modern computers they used within the Federation. She told her tech to photograph it from every angle before removing it to the surface. At the door to exit the quarters, she took a deep breath and stepped into the place she feared most. But as she walked the one hundred and thirty meters to the open cavern, she began to feel lighter in her heart.

There were people looking out for her, and her team. The tunnel was shored up in the oddest locations, but those were shored up because the experts, the Engineers determined if a failure was to occur, there was the location and they were not going to allow anyone to get hurt due to their negligence.

When she reached the surface his aircar was gone, so she just went to her desk in the research facility where she found a note telling her they would have dinner that evening at 1900 hours at the Marine Mess.

Tonight would be in a sense their second date so Emily went to her quarters earlier than normal, showered, and changed from her working jumpsuit to slacks and a simple pull-over blouse. She brushed her hair out thinking she might have it cut since it was nearly to the middle of her back. A dab of Honeysuckle fragrant perfume, and she was set for the evening.

Ezra arrived carrying something flat and wrapped in a red cloth. Once they had gone through the buffet line and taken a table away from everyone else, he slid the object over to her. She carefully unwrapped what turned out to be a picture frame, but there was no photo in it. What she saw was the badges and emblems of a Lancer.

"Emily, you said you wanted to know who I am. I told you today you had to defeat your fears to know me. You took that first step today and tonight, I give you a part of me that is known, but still unknown if you understand what I am telling you. That is a piece of my life, of who I am. Today is only the beginning. But to add a caveat to our agreement, you can never tell anyone what I tell you until I decide it is time to tell the universe. If you cannot promise me that, then tonight is the end, not the beginning."

"Are you telling me you're in love with me?"

"No Emily, but I'm tired of running. I'll make you this promise. If love does develop between us, both of us, then I will give you the universe."

"What makes you think that I won't declare my love for you just to get the universe?"

"I have no defense against that except I believe you are not that kind of woman. Otherwise you would have married the man you were engaged to for nearly three years."

Emily laughed at that statement before responding.

"Alright Ezra, I promise not to speak of your past to anyone without your permission. Does that put us back on track?"

"Yes, now eat before it gets cold."

During dinner, Ezra explained each piece in the frame, what they meant without going into gory details of most of them. Emily did ask several questions and when she noticed him seeming to balk at answering one question, she told him not to answer if it made him uncomfortable.

Once more after dinner he escorted her to her quarters and tonight like before they kissed, this time longer and firmer. When she entered her quarters she turned back to Ezra.

"I detest being pawed over, and you have been a perfect gentleman. But that does not mean you can't touch in a gentle way."

Ezra chuckled over the comment. Two nights later he gripped her buttock with one hand and squeezed her hard, pulling her tighter to him and heard her moan from the contact.

They would go as many as four nights without seeing one another and each time he only gripped her with one hand. During the days, he watched her take greater steps in overcoming her fear of the roof falling in until he noticed she walked around the site as if she was on a transport or within a building, without fear of the roof falling in.

That night he presented her with another frame showing his Fleet service, but he withheld the Medal of Valor from her as it was the final string to his past. Later they did not just kiss, they made out like a couple of hormone raging teenagers with his hands gently moving about her body and her hands digging her fingers into his back at times. When they finally broke up she told him she was going to take a cold shower and suggested he did the same. He could only laugh as she was rubbing his crotch at the time feeling the firmness contained in his pants. She could still hear him laughing after she closed the door on him then leaned back against it to catch her breath.

The next morning Ezra received a message he was needed back on Nemea to close a deal that had been in the works before the discovery of the cavern. He found Emily at her desk and showed her the message so she would know he was not leaving of his own will, and told her he'd be back as soon as he closed the deal and had all the paperwork in order.

Emily walked to his aircar with him, and the kiss was one of lover's departing. She watched as he flew back to his cabin where his shuttle would pick him up thinking two weeks seemed a lifetime at this point in their relationship. She knew she was in love with him, but was it true love or just the desire to be with him?

As Ezra boarded his shuttle, his only thoughts were of returning to Emily and if she spoke the words he needed to hear, he would bare his soul to her. Not to get her into bed, but to bring her into his heart.

Discovery

For Emily, the time without Ezra being near seemed an eternity. Every time she entered the tunnels, she thought about how much faith Ezra showed in her and how he forced her to face her fears, and with every twinge of apprehension she felt, she drew upon the thought she could not let him down.

Ezra's problem was with the transit times between planets. There was only so much to do then the rest of the time was wasted in thought about where he wanted to be, and who he wanted to be with.

On Nemea, Ezra threw himself into closing the deal he had been working on so he could return to Emily. Before he had left for Hildur, he had placed a bid on a trace of land which was already under ownership that had failed due to the settler's sponsors backing out due to their worries with the operation so close to unknown space.

The on again, off again war along the Eastern Rim, the discovery of a new race by Carlos Gannaway, the Princess Consuela's nephew, then the disappearance of several prospector's near Nemean space spooked off a lot of investors, even though the Fleet had a strong presence in the region.

What started off as a bid to obtain an additional four thousand hectares, ended up with Ezra holding title to nearly seven thousand hectares of both farmland and forested ground. He decided to wait until the Hildur cavern operation was closed before he made his decision about what to do with the new land. The hay business was tampering off as planets recovered from their droughts, but he was not going to waste the grass on this new land and instructed Simon to take charge of that operation, and store the hay for future use or sales.

Lieutenant Horner walked up to Emily as she was examining what appeared to be a toy lying on one of the examination tables in the Research Facility.

"Doctor Lee, Mister Connors ship has entered orbit. He should be on the ground within the hour."

Emily suddenly lost all interest in the toy as she looked up at Horner trying to keep her eyes from misting over.

"Thank you Lieutenant. If anyone wants me, I'll be at his office to greet him when he lands."

Horner smiled a knowing smile, then gave her a two finger salute before walking away. Emily pulled her sterile gloves off and walked over to her chief research assistant and told him the same thing before going out to the car park and taking one of their aircars to his office. She had several questions to ask him and she wanted to be alone with him when she asked them.

Ezra stepped off the shuttle ramp to see Emily sitting on his porch steps a hundred meters away. His stomach seemed to do a flip as walked towards her, and his focus was so narrow, he never heard the shuttle lift to return to his ship. As he closed with her, he had a moment of panic in that maybe she had decided to end what relationship they had while he was away.

Emily stood and looked at the man she knew she wanted more than life itself, but she also had concerns he would not want her in that manner. She knew from his file that he had lovers on Nemea. Had he visited one of more of them while gone?

He was about three meters from the porch steps when she stopped him with her raised hand.

"Ezra Connors, I am in love with you. Was that message you showed me a real message, or one made up as an excuse for you to leave and force me into facing my demons alone, and the fact I want you in my life?"

"No Emily, it was real and I have the paperwork in my satchel to prove it. And Emily, I too discovered I am in love with you, more than I have ever loved anyone in my life."

"Then Mister Connors, take me to your bed because who you were in the past no longer concerns me. I only want the man in front of me, not the man he once was."

"They are the same man Emily, only with a different label."

He stepped to her, placed his bags on the porch, then grabbed her by her buttocks, pulling her to him as tight as humanly possible. She moaned as they kissed with him pulling her up to his level then she wrapped her legs around his waist as he held her in place. When the kiss was broken, she laid her head on his shoulder, as he bent over and retrieved his bags, then stepped up on the porch.

She just held onto him as if he was a piece of drift wood to save herself from drowning in a sea of emotions. He was able to thumb his door lock open, then stepped inside the cabin, dropped his bags and kicked the door closed with his foot. He took her to his bed and leaned over so he could place her onto it.

Emily released her hold on him as he stood back up looking down at her while unfastening his jacket. She rolled out of his way and got off the bed as she too was removing her clothing.

"Ezra, I need a shower first as I have been down in the tunnel twice today. I'll wash your back if you wash mine."

Once bare of all clothing it still took a while before they found the shower as they kissed and enjoyed the heat of flesh against each other. She washed more than his back and even dropped on him for a short time until he told her to stop or he would be wasted for several hours as he recovered.

In bed, more wet than dry, she wanted him to take her almost as soon as she felt the sheets against her back but he had no intention of moving that quick, and returned the favor she showed him in the shower. But when they finally coupled, she was loud in declaring her pleasure and he later admitted he lasted longer than he figured he would. She declared the activity a major success.

They spent the rest of the day in bed, leaning about each other, then taking dinner at the mess since he had been gone for sixteen days and his larder needed refreshing. Back again to his bed where she showed him how limber she was and then falling into an exhausted sleep.

The next morning started where they left off before showering again to wash the sweat and smell of sexual combat. Neither of them had any doubt about their feelings for each other at this point, and both knew how it would end as they separated to go to work.

That afternoon, Ezra flew Emily into Kankakee to find her an engagement ring. When he proposed to her over lunch, he told her that they should wait until the cavern project was at a point she could be away from it for a month or more for a honeymoon. She moved her personal belongings into his cabin that evening.

Three weeks after his return they were still making love like a couple of newlyweds that discovered gold in bed. He also discovered she was talented in other ways as she caught him in a dark corner one day down in the cavern and finished what she had started in the shower their first night together.

The Marines were opening new doors daily and exploring connecting tunnels as the investigation progressed. The Research Facility was nearly over worked with items coming out of the rooms for examination and testing of materials. The chairs brought out were uncomfortable for a human to sit on and the beds were oddly shaped for a human to lay upon. The materials the sheets and other cloth type materials were coarse and woven in a pattern never seen before. Plus the material was all synthetic and fire resistant.

The warehouse was becoming cramped with items brought up from the rooms and the research technicians began to only bring up what was new and unseen before, leaving the rest of the objects in the room after carefully photographing the entire room. Each inspected room was then sealed and marked as being investigated.

One thing that was bothering Emily about these rooms was the lack of eating utensils or food preparation facilities. Where or how were these aliens eating, and where was that facility located?

The Marines estimated they still had several kilometers of tunnels to open for investigation as tunnels connected with tunnels.

Marines being somewhat paranoid when dealing with things they did not understand, had established a warning system throughout the tunnel complex which could be activated by any Marine through his battle helmet. It had been tested and everyone, especially the civilians understood not to ignore any warning coming through the system and to evacuate the complex immediately. That is except for the Marines who would move to the location of the warning.

It was nine months after the project started that the warning system came alive as the Marines opened another room. Ezra was sitting at his desk in his cabin/office going over the accounts of his business on Hildur when the small receiver on his desk came alive. He had it there for situations like this where he was off-site.

All the warning gave was to evacuate the complex immediately without giving any specifications on why it was necessary. Ezra grabbed his helmet, vest, and carbine as he headed for the door and his aircar. When he landed at the site, he saw Emily taking a headcount of the civilians, and Marines positioned to keep anyone other than a Marine from entering the site.

He put on his vest then his helmet, telling his AI to link with the Marines frequency so he could listen in on any conversation being conducted. It was when he was walking over to Emily that he finally learned why the complex was sealed. A body had been found in one of the rooms.

"Emily, do you have everyone?"

"Yes Ezra. All are accounted for." She spoke while checking the personnel roster on her pad. "Do you know why we had to evacuate?"

He took her arm and moved her away from the crowd of people.

"From what I have heard," He tapped the side of his helmet. "The Marines have found a body in one of the rooms.

Keep everyone out here for now until I can find out more about what is going on."

"Okay Ezra, please be careful."

Ezra was hearing the cross talk between Lieutenant Horner and one of his Corpsmen concerning biohazards from the body. The Corpsman said his instruments did not pick up anything to be concerned about, but he wanted a Doctor down with more advanced equipment to test the air.

Horner did not hesitate in calling their transport and requesting a full Medical team down to check the complex and the civilians who had been working without any sort of breathing protection while inside the complex.

Ezra jogged to the stairs and took them two at a time as he descended into the complex then jogged towards the location of the room with the body in it. The Marines in the tunnels never questioned his being there and directed him from one tunnel to another in the maze of the complex. As he entered one tunnel he met Horner entering from another and together they jogged towards their objective.

When they arrived at the room, the door was closed with a Marine outside it.

"Who's in there?" Horner demanded.

"Parker, and Doc Wingo."

"Alright, stand aside and let no one else in."

"Yes Sir."

The room was lit with flares and Ezra saw the Corpsman standing near the bed with what appeared to be a body on it. The Marine, Parker, was standing off to the side looking away from the body.

"Parker, you alright?" Horner asked.

"Yes Sir, just kind of shook up is all. Sure didn't expect to find a body after all this time down here."

"Understand Marine. Try to relax and we'll get you out of here as soon as the Doc clears you."

"He can go Lieutenant, I find nothing to be worried about here."

"Alright then Parker, get topside and get some fresh air, but do not speak of this to anyone, not even Doctor Lee, understand?"

"Yes Sir."

Parker left, nearly running out the door. Ezra stood looking at the body feeling his guts tighten up as the Corpsman moved away giving him a better view of the corpse on the bed. After all the years running away from his past, he finally came face to face with one of the creatures that killed his crew.

"Mister Connors...... Mister Connors!"

It was Horner trying to get his attention.

"What? Yeah, Lieutenant, what?"

"Sir, are you going to shoot that corpse?"

Ezra looked down at the grip he had on his carbine and the position it was being held. The muzzle was pointed at the body on the bed.

"Sorry. Lieutenant Horner in case you are not aware of it. That creature on the bed is of the same race that we have been at war with along the Eastern Rim. Contact the Fleet and let them know about this immediately."

"Are you sure of this Mister Connors?"

Ezra stood looking at the body.

"At one time it was Commander and yes, I am sure."

"Frack! Let's go Doc, we're sealing this room. Mister Connors, please evacuate this room. I think you've seen enough today."

"Yeah Lieutenant, I've seen more than enough."

Ezra left the room and told his AI to close all communications as he heard Horner began to issue orders, then contact his transport with instructions to advise the Fleet what they had found. He was lost in thought and if not for the Marines positioned at tunnel junctures, he might have wandered deeper into the complex.

He knew what he had to do now and there was no way to prevent it from happening. Full exposure of his identity was the last step to clear his conscious of having survived when his crew was killed. Above ground was the woman he intended to marry and he had to protect her from harm in case they found more aliens, especially alive aliens deeper into the complex.

Ezra caught up with Horner at the cavern entrance and it looked like he was arguing with someone over his comm system. Ezra had his AI reconnect so he could listen in. It sounded like the folks in orbit were giving him trouble about sending the message to the Fleet plus asking for more men on the ground. He broke into the conversation.

"This is Fleet Commander Eli Decker, Fleet reserve. Get those Marines on the ground now, and notify Fleet Sector Headquarters of our situation here. Do this now, or my next transmission will be to the Throne!"

There was a long pause before he received a response.

"Commander Decker was killed in a test flight. Who is this?"

"I'll say this only once. Your medical people can pull my DNA and confirm my identity once on the ground. Now execute my orders before you find yourself flying a trash hauler around Phoebes."

Horner slide his face shield up and looked at Ezra.

"You really Commander Decker?"

"Yeah Lieutenant, I am. And before you say another word, I'm no hero, just a survivor."

Ezra walked away from Horner and headed up the stairs to the surface. Topside he stood looking at Emily standing with her people and knew that today was the day she would learn the truth about the man she was going to marry. As he was covering the nearly four hundred meters to her, he received a message from the transport.

"Commander Decker, do you copy, over?"

"Yes, I copy, go ahead, over."

"Stand by for a retrans, over."

The next voice he heard was of a female. One he had hoped to never hear again.

"Commander, are you sure you want to do this?"

"No, but I must ensure that the people here are safe. What are your orders Your Highness?"

"I am ordering three Fleets into the region from the interior. I am also dispatching a Lancer Task Force directly to Hildur to be placed under your command once on the ground to search the complex to insure no living alien is present to cause you and the people there any danger. I hereby elevate you to the rank of Commodore and place you in command of the Fleets assets within the region. Your mission is to protect the Federation subjects within the region. Do you accept your promotion and assignment?"

"Your Highness is playing on my dedication to the Federation and guilt. But yes, I accept, but once this mission is over, and the people secure, you know what my response will be to any additional orders."

Laughter came over the speakers in his helmet.

"My dear husband heard your remarks and advised that he will gladly execute those particular instructions for you. May the Saints protect and guide you Commodore Decker."

"One last thing Your Highness. Elevate Lieutenant Horner to Captain and assign him as my aide."

"It shall be done, Commodore."

The signal was broken at that point and he once again looked at Emily. He waved for her to come to him as he walked to her. They met away from her people and he took his helmet off, and looked at her before speaking.

"Emily, have you ever heard of Eli Decker?"

"Everyone from Earth has heard of Eli Decker. Why are you asking me that?"

"Because I am Eli Decker. I have been running from my past and with help from certain people have taken the identity of Ezra Connors. Even my death was designed to allow me to run away from my past."

"How did you get such a clean past? I mean even Federation Intelligence was involved."

"Because the pilot I saved the day I got my crew killed was Prince Randolph, heir to the Throne. I didn't know that at the time, I only knew I had to protect a pilot from being killed in his ejection pod."

"Why are you telling me this now?"

"Because Eli Decker is once more alive in the universe, and I am now responsible for the lives of you, and everyone on this planet and in this sector. The Throne has promoted me to Commodore and laid those responsibilities in my lap."

"Again, why?"

"Because what the Marines found down below. They found the body of an alien. The body of the aliens we are at war with along the Eastern Rim. Emily, all research stops at this point as far as the interior of the complex is concerned until we can be certain there are no living aliens to cause a single member of your team harm. I hate doing this, but my concern is for your safety, and that of your people."

"I understand Ezra, or do I call you Eli now?"

"The universe will soon know they are one and the same. I'll let you choose which one you wish to marry since all of my business dealings is as Ezra Connors."

"I fell in love with Ezra Connors and promised to marry him. Eli Decker is a great man, a hero to millions, but his time was only a moment in history, where Ezra Connors has built an empire through hard worked over time. No, our children will be raised as Connors when the time comes."

"So it shall be. Now go brief your people and get them back to work. If anyone left anything in the complex they must recover, find a Marine and have them contact me before going back into the complex under escort. One last thing, there is a Lancer Task Force enroute here to take over the Marines assignment. They will clear the complex before any more investigation by you or your people."

"Ezra…"

"No argument my love, in this my word is final. This is not a family matter in which I will welcome debate."

"Yes dear. I can accept that. Now it looks like Lieutenant Horner is trying to get your attention."

Ezra pulled Emily to him and kissed her before turning to deal with Horner.

"Go Em, do as I asked."

She just smiled and returned to her people as he waved Horner over to him.

Horner approached, paused for a second then saluted Ezra.

"Commodore Decker, I have received orders making me your aide during this period of emergency."

"Captain, I am not comfortable with the title Commodore or the name Decker. But I was born with one and royally appointed the other. Pull the Engineers out of the complex and once the Battalion is on the ground, we're going to work securing the complex until the Lancers get here. Right now I'm going to contact Isaac and have a crew come in and build us a headquarters so we have someplace to work. As your Marines pull out, have them lace the complex already explored with intrusion devices. Now go and get this done."

"Yes Sir." Horner just nodded as a salute and took off at a jog, calling for his Gunny and senior Sergeants.

An hour later the lead elements of the orbiting Infantry Battalion landed to find Ezra bent over the front of his aircar looking at a topographical map of the region. With the Battalion came the medical team he had ordered. Ezra told them to go into the complex with coverage by the Marines that had already been in the complex, and determine if they can safely retrieve the body for autopsy, and if possible, a determination of how long it had laid there.

Ezra then pointed out to the Marine Battalion Commander that this complex lay in a valley with steep hills on both sides. He wanted patrols in those hills to see if they could visually find any location that aliens may move in and out of the complex just in case they had missed something underground.

He reminded the Marines that their sensors could not pick up on the materials used to construct the complex, so the Assault Boat sensors were basically worthless. It was boots on the ground, but to keep the boats on standby in case of need.

Once the Marines went to work, all Ezra could do at this point was wait. He could not push the Marines any harder than he already had, and until Isaac arrived with a crew and materials, there was no real place for him to just sit and wait.

Lancers!

Ezra went looking for Emily as it seemed he suddenly did not have anything to do once he had issued his orders. Marines were landing and moving out along the ridges and valley walls to search for anything that might be of danger to all personnel in the valley.

He found her in the Research Facility at her desk.

"Em, I don't have time at the moment, but would you go to the cabin, gather your things and pack me a simple bag and bring them back here. We're going to have to use your quarters until I am certain the situation here is stable enough to return to the cabin at night."

"Sure Ezra, I'll go do that now. Please be careful."

"You too Em."

A quick peck on the lips then he headed back out to observe the events taking place around the complex. He didn't make it far when he was approached by a Fleet Senior Lieutenant wearing a muted grey splotched battle uniform.

"Commodore Decker, I'm Senior Lieutenant Bronson. I've been ordered by Fleet Sector Headquarters to your staff as aide or whatever tasks needs accomplished, sir."

Ezra looked at the neatly turned out Lieutenant then smiled.

"Lieutenant, your first task is to get me properly uniformed since this is the uniform of a Lancer. It will be complete and battle ready, understood?"

"Aye Sir, understood."

Ezra gave the Lieutenant the sizes of his trousers, jacket, and such then watched him walk away as the Lieutenant was talking on a separate Fleet frequency to the ship aloft.

He saw a tall Marine just walking around the area with a wooden staff taller than he was as if lost. Ezra walked over to him taking notice of everything about him, wondering who he was. When the Marine happened to turn in his direction, Ezra had to smile as the Marine was a Lieutenant Commander wearing the symbol of a Chaplin.

"Father, are you lost?" Ezra asked him as he approached.

"No my son, I was looking at the soil here. It's rich, perfect for farming."

"Father, I'm Decker, do you have a few minutes to talk?"

"Commodore, I always have time to talk to a member of the flock. What is troubling you Commodore?"

Ezra described how he had been running from the truth of his guilt. His survivor's guilt all these years and how it had effected his feelings towards others. But in finding Emily, he had faced those fears and the pain of carrying them.

"Commodore, you are not special in this. I have consoled many Marines over the years for the same ailment, but you have to remember, the Saints have a purpose in letting one man die and another live. Maybe this is your purpose here on Hildur, or maybe there is another place you are needed. I did a bit of research before dropping and it seems you have brought prosperity to both Hildur and Nemea. Maybe that is the purpose they have for you. Only time will tell."

"Father, I have never been a religious man, but I do concern myself with Karma and the myth of the Fates. Could they also be the Saints in another form?"

The Chaplin laughed.

"Commodore, I have had that same thought many times and to be honest, I think they are all one and the same, only called such according to our anger and frustration with life in general."

They stood quietly for a moment before the Chaplin placed his hand on Ezra's shoulder.

"Commodore, I imagine that when you went to save that pilot from being killed in his escape pod, all you considered was that pilot's life. I would be willing to bet you figured on getting in then out before you suffered too much damage, then found yourself in a tempest that you could not escape from so you placed yourself between the aliens and the escape pod so others could retrieve it. Yes, a moment of miscalculation has followed you all these years, but your intentions were clear and honorable. We are all human and make mistakes which we must live with if we survive."

"Thank you Father. Now one other thing."

The next day, Ezra and Emily were married by the Chaplin with Isaac standing as his best man and one of Emily's female research technicians as her maid of honor in front of the Research Facility with a large crowd in attendance. He was in the uniform of a Fleet Commodore while she was dressed in the best clothes she had available.

He promised her they would take a long vacation once the situation was settled and could depart Hildur and go where ever she desired. She told him she wanted to go to the Swiss Alps on Earth and learn to ski as that was one childhood dream she had never been able to accomplish. And that she would not become pregnant until that dream was realized. He just smiled and told her they would practice making babies until then.

The Fleets that Princess Consuela ordered into the region began arriving, reporting for assignment. Ezra just assigned them portions of the sector rim and told them to venture as deep as they felt was safe. The Fleets on this side of the Federation had yet to be equipped with the newest Scout Ships which were better armored, protected than the ones he once flew, so he advised the Fleet Commanders to use them sparingly.

Four days after the wedding, the Lancer Task Force arrived. With the Task Force came his old Regiment, the Seventh, and the Battalion Commander had been a Company Commander when he was a member. The reunion with men he once knew was

117

short, and at times bitter as it brought back memories best left forgotten.

Ezra laid out a diagram of the known tunnels and told the Lancer Command to just start at one end and don't stop until the entire complex was located and diagrammed out. He pointed out five places that the Marines had found air ventilation shafts, but those shafts were too small for even the size of the aliens.

Every opened room was to be photographed before closing and marking it as being inspected. Any additional bodies would be immediately reported so Fleet Medical personnel could removed them.

The Lancers assigned a Gunnery Sergeant who was on limited duty to Ezra as liaison during this mission. Ezra knew the Gunny from his time when the man was just a Private. It was then that Ezra recognized he was needing additional help and had the Fleet assign him two Yeomen from the ships over Hildur to help handle the paperwork that was beginning to pile up on his desk.

One thing the Lancers brought that Ezra had forgotten about were small, four man electric carts powered by small fusion bottles and they lowered six of them down into the cavern and utilized them in moving people around, plus two were staged as a reaction force of eight Lancers.

It was the Lancer Tunnel Rats and Sappers that moved through the tunnels, looking for any signs of danger with the Infantry moving in behind them, opening doors and clearing the rooms before moving on.

Two weeks into the search by the Lancers, the Marines who were still sweeping the hills in a grid manner reported something out of the ordinary along the Eastern ridge, about half way down. It was a large, bare area where no trees were growing and the grass looked stunted. The location was marked on the topographical map then estimated where it should be in relation to tunnel complex. The Tunnel Rats went to work moving through the complex, looking for anything which might lead to that bare spot.

Ezra was confused by the fact they had opened over three hundred rooms up to date and yet to find a mess facility, or any type of communications center. Even if the diet of the aliens was greatly different from humans, there should be signs of eating, even in the rooms used as quarters. There was waste disposal systems, but no food preparation systems to be found. The autopsy report on the body reported grains in what was estimated to be the stomach of the dead alien, but how or why it died was still unknown even with the data the Fleet had from bodies recovered on the Eastern Rim after a battle.

Emily and her research team were finally allowed to reenter the complex with Lancer escorts but were kept far back from where the current searches were taking place. She too was perplexed by the lack of specific items which would normally be found in the quarters of the average human.

Then Emily posted a comment to the main assignment board in the Research Facility: Why was this one body found in quarters and no other bodies have been located?

Ezra sent a message to the Throne asking for all medical information the Fleet held on the recovered bodies of Aliens from the Eastern Rim for Emily and her team to examine, especially the classified reports.

It would be two weeks before they saw the reports and with them came an Altairian Medical team which specialized in Genetics.

The Tunnel Rats were opening tunnels far beneath the Eastern Ridge and had yet to find any manner of access upwards. It was when one of the Infantry teams who were opening the rooms behind the Tunnel Rats discovered the way up when they opened a room that things began to fall into place.

The door they opened did not lead them into a room but into an elevator, as did the door across the hall. Photos were taken of the symbols on those specific doors and each Lancer had a copy in hand. At this point, the opening of rooms ceased as the search for other doors with those markings took the highest priority.

119

It took the Marine and Lancer Engineers several days to determine how to power the elevators then what the symbols on the controls meant. The elevators would only hold four men, and once Ezra gave the go ahead, eight Lancers went to the top of the elevator shaft to find themselves in an underground hanger.

The hanger was empty except for a single craft that appeared to be under repair when abandoned. What appeared to be the hanger doors to the outside world were stuck shut so the Lancers used a breaching charge to blow through them as if they were breaching a hatch on a space vessel.

The hole they blew through one door was large enough for a man to step through and the Marines outside had cleared the area during this experiment. Sunlight came though the hole and then as the dust settled, so did a Marine to let them know they had discovered why the spot was so bare outside.

Now there was another mystery to solve. Who or when was the hanger doors covered with soil, and why were they covered?

Also according to the elevator controls, there were at least three more levels between the tunnel complex and the hangers.

Ezra did not like sending only eight Lancers at a time into the unknown, but was uncertain how to deal with that specific problem. It was Horner that told the truth why Ezra was having problems determining how to deal with that problem.

"Commodore, the problem as I see it is that you are afraid of losing people to the unknown. But let's be realistic here. The moment we raised our hands, and then signed our enlistment papers, each of us have been living on borrowed time. No one wants to die, and we all know we'll never live forever, so we do the job we signed up for and hope for the best. With all due respect Commodore, get your head out of the past and get on with the program."

Ezra sat looking at Horner for several minutes, no emotion showing on his face then he turned to his Lancer Gunny.

"Pickens, send word to the Lancers to open those other levels. How they do it is up to them, but let's get them opened for investigation."

Pickens never replied, he just moved over to the communications console and issued the orders. All they could do now was wait for the results. Ezra was silently praying no one would get hurt because of his orders. All Ezra could do was wait for the reports to come in from the Lancers. This was the worst part, the waiting.

As the Lancers were preparing to open the other levels, the Marines took it upon themselves to open the hanger doors wider, so if needed, they could flow through to support the Lancers from above. They carefully removed the sides of the elevator shaft and rigged ropes in case they had to slide down them to assist the Lancers below them.

Two hours after Ezra gave the order, the level below the hanger was opened. This was the command center, the headquarters they had been looking for. The Lancers checked the area carefully looking for hidden panels which an enemy could pop out of before dropping to the next level.

Here they found what they suspected to be a medical facility but the Lancer Medic who was part of the team reported nothing look familiar or useable in reference to a human. Again, it was searched before dropping to the last level to be open.

This area was much larger than the other levels as it appeared this was their mess facility. Based upon a rough count of seating and calculations, it could hold upwards of three hundred individuals at a time. The Lancers quickly used up all of their Chem-Flares and waited until more could be brought to them before they did a wall to wall search of the facility.

It was near what they considered to be the kitchen they found four more bodies lying on the floor as if they had fallen from their chairs as death took them. They found another two bodies in the kitchen itself, lying between what may have been stoves. The Lancers just backed out of the area once they could confirm no other bodies were present, nor were there any live aliens to cause them trouble.

Now it was up to the scientists and medical personnel to deal with the bodies.

Possibilities

The Tunnel Rats returned to their routine once the elevator was discovered and those additional levels were opened. It would have been easy for them to become complacent as they moved through the darkness of the tunnels looking for trouble but even as clean and barren as the tunnels were, they were experienced in discovering trouble when they least expected it. This made their work slow as a snail's pace at times.

Now with photos of the symbols for the elevators, they focused on finding other elevators and not just bypassing doors for the Infantry to open and discover what was behind them. In doing so, they found six more elevators. But these went down, not up.

Ezra sat looking at the diagram of the tunnel complex pinned to the wall of his headquarters trying to determine an sense of logic to it. There was none.

Then there was the fact that if you remove dirt for a tunnel, you have to place it somewhere else. But there were no mounds of dirt within a thousand kilometers to indicate any such activity. It was known that the aliens mined asteroids, could they have been mining this world, and the tunnels were following the minerals through the soil?

But why haven't they discovered a shaft upwards into the valley itself? A manner to remove the soil and debris from the mining. It was suggested that since they had yet to discover any manner of smelting or removing the minerals they may have been mining, every ounce of material removed from the tunnels, and rooms were taken elsewhere for processing. That was a more viable explanation than any other theories being postulated.

Emily's research team had been supplemented by nearly two dozen additional experts in various fields, and the housing, mess facilities and additional buildings for research was expanding into a small city. Roads were built into the valley to support traffic from Kankakee bringing in supplies almost daily to support the efforts of the researchers and military.

There was one event which Ezra thought as somewhat comical at the time and placed Emily in a position she did not care for, yet was intended to make her life easier.

The Fleet Admiral for the Northern Sector arrived for an inspection tour since it was under Fleet control and protection. The military side of the operation was well in hand with Ezra dealing with both the Marines and Lancers, but there seemed to the Admiral a lot of confusion on the research side not understanding how scientists operated in their specific fields, plus having military specialists working alongside the civilians.

He used a vague regulation within the Federation Fleet regulations to appoint Emily a Full Commander within the Fleet placing the military specialists under her command, with her under Ezra's command.

Emily thought this was nonsense since there were no problems between any of the scientists and specialists working for her that was not resolved through dialogue between the parties involved. Often it was nothing more than a misunderstanding of definitions in the course of the investigations being conducted.

She told the Admiral what she thought about his idea.

"Admiral, from the very beginning, the Commodore and I have had a good working relationship. The Marines and Lancers who work side by side with my people also have a good working relationship. Your Fleet specialists also have a good working relationship with their counterparts on my team. Now I spend the nights under the Commodore, and you want me under him during the day at work? If this causes a divorce, I'm naming you as a principal to it."

The Admiral was shocked by her statements until she laughed and let him off the hook.

"Admiral, thank you for the honor, but it is not necessary."

Once he regained his composure, he replied to her comments.

"Doctor Lee, excuse me, Doctor Connors, I think you will find that you will no longer have to go through the Commodore, your husband to obtain additional help or equipment. Once the orders are published and distributed, all commands within this sector will respond to your requests, plus my headquarters will immediately forward requests to Fleet if we are not able to provide you with the assets you need without having to bother the Commodore, who has his hands full with the military side of this operation."

"Thank you Admiral. We'll try not to be any more of a burden than we already are."

When the Admiral suggested that she be assigned two Yeomen to assist her, she was specific that they be medical or scientific trained Yeomen so she would not be wasting time having to explain terms to them a standard Yeomen such as the Commodore utilized. The Admiral agreed to her request and his aide sent out a request for volunteers from those fields. Within an hour, there were over two dozen volunteers signed up for the chance to work on Hildur.

Ezra was standing in a tunnel observing the Lancers disassemble an elevator since they could not get it to power up. They were going to drop down the shaft on ropes to the next level before dropping again to the level below that. Once again Ezra was worried about losing people to the unknown. It seemed a contradiction to his Lancer days but back then, he led and they followed, now he ordered and they went.

The elevator had symbols for three levels and once the Lancers felt they were ready slide down the ropes, they dropped Chem-flares down the shaft. What they got in return was not the sound of a solid object hitting a floor, but a splashing sound. Looking down, the flares were floating on water. This was the first indication of a water source within the complex.

In looking down the shaft and counting the obvious levels from the platforms in the shaft, there were two more levels than marked on the elevator controls with the water level being one of them. This caused the Lieutenant in charge of the Tunnel Rats to back the operation up until they could get a remote camera down the shaft to see into each level.

It was nearly two hours before the cameras were in place and lowered down to the next level. The cameras were low powered, designed for looking into small spaces such as on a ship so what the people operating them saw was only clear for about twenty meters in front of the lens. Beyond that, everything blurred out.

Also the cameras operated in the Infrared instead of the white light spectrum which added to the distortion.

Ezra watched on the cameras monitor as the Lancer operator tried to get a better focus until he just gave up and apologized for the failure of the equipment to function beyond its design. Ezra looked over at the Tunnel Rats awaiting their orders to go down the ropes, then looked at the ropes hanging in the elevator, walked over, stepped onto the lip of the shaft, grabbed a rope and slid down to the next level. Above him he could hear several people make exclamations concerning what they had just witnessed, then he felt the sensation of another person on the rope above him.

He stopped sliding at the level entrance, placed a foot on the lip on the entrance, then grabbed the side of the entrance with his hand and pulled himself into the level, clearing the way for the next individual. Even wearing his helmet, he was basically blind at this point due to the nature of the darkness within the room.

Suddenly a Chem-flare came flying through the access from the elevator shaft, lighting the area and Ezra suddenly felt frightened by what he was seeing in the distance. The next person through the door was a female Centaurian Tunnel Rat, and she was not polite in her comments to him.

"Damn it Commodore, what the frack do you think you are doing dropping in like that!"

Ezra looked at her as she was bracing him, grabbed her and turned her towards what was in this room which was actually a cavern extending beyond his visual range. She stood there, then gasped at what was before her. They heard another person drop into the room and a moment later they let out an exclamation.

"Holy Frack!"

Extending out before them was what appeared to be row after row of Alien's planted in soil with their heads above the surface. Now the question in Ezra's mind was this a cemetery, or a garden? One of the major questions the scientist had yet to discover was the reproductive processes within the bodies of the Aliens they had autopsied.

Ezra keyed his helmets radio.

"Commander Connors, link your monitor to my signal, over."

It took a moment before she responded since transmitters were required this far into the complex.

"Go ahead Commodore, we're linked."

Ezra activated his helmets camera, transmitting the video to her monitor. He never spoke as he did this, just waited for her response.

"Oh my God Ezra! Get out of there! Get out now!"

"Sorry Em, but we need to know if they are dead or a danger to us. Either way, it needs to be dealt with."

He started moving towards the first row of heads, hoping the Lancers were following or at least preparing for a fight. This was something no one could have anticipated and certainly never trained for. He stopped just outside of arms reach with his carbine pointing down at the head in front of him. Something didn't look right about the skin of the creature.

Ezra squatted down and looked closer at the head sticking out of the ground. Even if he could reach the neck, he had no idea how to check for a pulse if they even had one. But there was mold growing on the head. A sickly red mold completely covering it.

He pulled his large knife from his leg sheath and tapped the top of the head with it. No reaction. He tapped it harder and the skull indented from the impact. Still no reaction. This Alien was dead, but again, was this a cemetery or a garden?

Stepping back as he stood up, Ezra looked at other heads and they all had the red mold on them. He took another step backwards and turned towards the access, seeing other Lancers had entered the cavern and all were positioned to provide him with fire support if necessary.

"Ezra?"

"Yes Emily?"

"Do not return to the complex level until a Decon unit can be set up."

"Yeah, no problem Em. Just don't take long will you. This place can get on your nerves real quick like."

"It's on its way now."

He walked back to the others, for no other reason than to be near a human at this time.

"Commodore, this is something out of a nightmare. What do we do if they rise up out of the ground?"

"Unless I'm grossly mistaken, they are dead, but just in case I'm wrong, we start laying down fire as the others climb back out of here even if the Decon unit is not ready for us. Go out in the order you came in while the rest of us covers them."

"Commodore, but you were the first in. With all due respect sir, get you ass out of here first, we'll cover you."

"Is that an order trooper?"

"In this case it is Commodore."

Ezra patted the Lancer on the shoulder and laughed.

He never said another word as they waited for the call to come back up to the main level. For over two hours they stood, waiting for the call, waiting for one of the Aliens to crawl out of the ground and come for them. No one spoke in the deathly silence of the cavern as they listened for signs of danger beyond their visual range.

When the call came, everyone actually jumped from the sound in their helmets speakers.

"Commodore, your first, come on up."

Ezra recognized Horner's voice in his helmet.

"On my way."

Before he stepped to the ropes he turned back to the others.

"Thanks for covering my dumb ass down here. Once through Decon, everyone is out of the cavern and off duty for the next twenty-four hours. Now let's do this quick and orderly."

He stepped to the ropes and even though it had been years since he had free climbed ropes, it seemed to come back to him the moment his hands touched the rope. Up he went as quick as he could because going up meant only one person at a time, and he had six people waiting their turn below him.

Decon was set up connected to the elevator access, sealed to prevent anything from further entering the complex. Technicians dressed in Level Five protection gave him a complete sensor reading, then sprayed him with a powered decontamination agent. Next he stepped into a second chamber, and into a collection tub where he was sprayed down from above with another agent, before moving to the next chamber to be air dried then given a bath of Ultra-violet light to kill any remaining agent he may have picked up. The last chamber was another check by sensors before he was allowed to exit the Decon station to find himself face to face with Emily.

"Commodore Decker, what is your opinion of what you found down there?"

"I have no opinions, only theories, but neither make sense at this time. But we are going to have to dig at least one of those creatures out before we know any more about that situation."

"I agree Commodore and depending on the analysis of the mold you found on the Alien, which I understand was on your clothing, we'll make plans accordingly."

"Sounds good Commander."

"Now Ezra, if you ever pull a stunt like that again, you can sleep in your office for the next week. You're a Commodore, not a Private, so stop acting like one. Do you hear me husband of mine?"

Ezra could only laugh before he could answer her.

"Yes my sweet Emily, I hear you loud and clear as I suspect half the complex did. I shall obey your orders as I have gotten use to the feel of your body at night. Now, you get your ass out of here and let these folks do their job."

She took his hand and led him to a cart, shoved him into a seat as he was laughing and told the driver to take them topside. With the introduction of the carts, the cavern opening had been widened and a ramp put in place so the carts could go in and out of the cavern.

It was some time later that Horner returned to the office with the field report on the mold they had taken off his uniform and the uniforms of the others. It appeared to be just that, mold, but until further tests in a lab could be made, there was no determination if it was hazardous to humans. Horner took Ezra's helmet over to the medical lab so the filters could be removed and further inspected, then have the filters replaced for future use.

Ezra thought he had enough troubles once back in his office after the chewing he had from Emily. She was still mad enough she did not give him a peck on the lips when they separated which she always did since their wedding. The next problem came through the door in the form of a gentleman from the Federation's Settler's Authority.

Bookkeeping

The gentleman who entered Ezra's office was named Herman Pendergrass, and he had came from New Brumsfield to see him about his quarterly tax reports, which had not been filed since the discovery of the complex and Ezra's duties overseeing the operations. Ezra had a minor panic attack when he realized he had been negligent in filing his taxes for both the Nemea and Hildur operations which were his responsibility, not one belonging to his business managers. And the penalties could be extremely stiff for failing to submit the reports.

"Mister Pendergrass, as you can see I have been distracted but I do not make that as an excuse. How bad is it going to be? The penalties I mean?"

"Oh, that is not why I am here. Granted, it has been noticed that you failed to submit the proper paperwork on schedule, but my purpose of being here is to assist you in preparing your forms during the duration of this operation on Hildur, to remove that burden from you Sir."

"Please don't take this wrong, but are you kidding me?"

"No Sir. In fact the Federation Council views this project, or operation, to be of the utmost importance to the Federation and completely understands how one could be distracted by it. All we have to do is get the paperwork brought up to date, see what taxes may need to be paid regardless of when due, then continue to keep the paperwork up to date until you are released from this assignment."

"Amazing Mister Pendergrass. Well, where do we start?"

"Commodore, all you have to do is to inform your managers to transmit facsimiles of all documents to me, and I'll get them sorted out. Who handles your payroll?"

"That is handled through the Exchequer. We submitted confirmation monthly and they pay my employees. My managers handle that transmittal by agreement with the Exchequer."

"Fine, that makes things easier. I shall only need copies of the Exchequers payment records which I can access from here once I have copies of the monthly confirmation forms. All I need now is a place to work."

"I have a cabin roughly twenty minutes by aircar from here. I'm staying on site right now so you can use the cabin as an office and quarters."

"Yes, they can work out nicely. I also understand you have recently married."

"Yes, that is correct."

"I'll need her financials also since she is legally your co-dependent, even if she is not listed on your business accounts. Unless you wish to file a declaration separating her from your businesses."

"No, but let me have one of my aides take you to talk to her as you can see, I have a pile of reports to deal with before we begin digging up the dead."

"Digging up the dead?"

"Yes Mister Pendergrass, it seems we have discovered an Alien cemetery, and our scientists, which my wife is head of, wants the bodies for examination."

"Oh my Lord. No one told me what was going on here on Hildur. Aliens you say? Oh my Lord."

Ezra had to restrain from laughing.

"Do not worry Mister Pendergrass, you'll be far away from that activity and we have a battalion of Marines, and a half Regiment of Lancers here protecting us from harm. Now if you go with my aide, Lieutenant Bronson, he will take you to meet my wife, and while gone I will message my managers here and on Nemea to transmit all required paperwork immediately."

After they had left, Horner smiled as he commented to Ezra that luck was on his side today. Ezra replied it wasn't so much luck as someone higher than the Federation Council was protecting his dumb ass for forgetting to file his business financials on time. He then told Horner to find a spare aircar and driver to move Mister Pendergrass around as needed.

Horner found a female Lancer who had been injured during a training exercise for off duty personnel to chauffeur Pendergrass around during his stay on Hildur.

Pendergrass tried not to bother Ezra or Emily any more than possible as he processed the paperwork to bring their business taxes up to date. He did noticed paperwork for labor and materials which Ezra had not had time to process, so he dealt with it, then moved on to the next item. Every time he brought in a monthly statement for Ezra to sign, he had to explain each item which at first bothered Ezra until he realized that Pendergrass was actually reducing his tax burden by utilizing tax breaks he was not aware of. From that point on, he paid close attention to what Pendergrass was doing with his books.

On the personal side, Pendergrass noted that Emily was still being paid by the university on New Brumsfield while now drawing the pay of a Fleet Full Commander. Ezra was still drawing a check every quarter as he had been since leaving the Fleet plus now a monthly check as a Commodore at nearly the top of the pay bracket based upon total years of service, even though he had a major break in said service. Nothing was said about the quarterly check since it was coded as non-taxable, non-reportable in the Exchequer system.

But as interesting as the distraction Pendergrass was providing, Ezra still needed to finish this mission and escape these surroundings. Another aspect of this mission was once it was determined this was an Alien site, and that there were thousands of duplicate artifacts, undamaged due to the environment or catastrophe, museums all over the Federation were begging for artifacts for display in their museums.

He turned that over to Emily since as far as he was concerned, the artifacts belonged in her arena, not his. Since every room in the complex was equipped the same, this made it simple for Emily. She just pick the best photos of the rooms, provided measurements of the rooms, plus a diagram of how the furniture or artifacts were placed in the room then sent them back to the requesting agency advising them they would be responsible for shipping to their museum.

She checked to make sure that providing said artifacts came under a Federation Grant, the only requirement she placed upon the receivers besides transportation, was the crating, packing and labor of such endeavors.

Ezra agreed with her to subcontract Isaac with him getting a local business license to cover the taxes and control the costs of preparing the items for shipment. Isaac had the lumber for the crates produced in the Connors mill and purchased them at wholesale, then he hired other men not employed by Ezra to do the labor at a decent wage. Once the first half dozen shipments were packed and ready for shipment, Isaac only had to bill the museum, collect the payment and pay the workers. Ezra loaned Isaac the money to insure the employees were paid until the payments came through, then Isaac repaid Ezra Crown for Crown with no interest.

It wasn't long before the warehouse was empty then Emily hired Isaac's employees as day labors, bringing up room after room and cleaning the artifacts separate what Isaac was paying them to package them for shipment. It stood to logic that Emily had to bring the items requested up for a museum, and such activities were covered in her operational funding, so between her and Isaac, they employed a dozen workers on a daily basis, both paying the same rate of pay so as not to confuse the system any more than possible.

Emily had Pendergrass look over the employee arrangement and determined it followed proper procedures even if it was a bit odd that the employee changed employers at a certain point in the process. But by Isaac buying the materials from the lumber mill he actually managed, it took Ezra and Emily out of that part of the equation. Any profit made from the packing materials was on Isaac's part, not theirs.

The Marine Engineers developed a dumb waiter system for the elevator to the graveyard as it was being called so the bodies could be lifted out once placed in a body bag. The graveyard was surveyed and each body given a number so later, it could be determined where the body was located in the graveyard.

But before Ezra allowed a single body to be removed, he wanted the other levels explored to insure that only dead Aliens existed within the complex. The dumb waiter could hold six Lancers and four more could ride on top of it. So as soon as the first six were off the waiter, it would drop and allow the other four to dismount, then hold in that position in case they had to make a hasty retreat from the level.

Ezra watched remotely from his office with Emily sitting next to him as a reminder of what she had told him about playing soldier again. There was a monitor for each person dropping into the next level. Ezra's stomach was knotting up as if he was making the drop himself as he watched the sides of the shaft go by then heads dropping to watch the top edge door frame appear. The head movements of each individual mimicked the others as they anticipated entering the next level.

As soon as able, flares were being tossed through the opening, lighting up the next level and it seemed as if everyone squatted just a bit so they could leave the confinement of the lift that much faster.

One ducked even further then launched themselves through the opening with the others following moments later. Soon the six were in the level tossing flares as far as possible while searching for a target which might harm them, except, it seemed this level was empty, barren of a single item to even trip over.

Soon the Lancers from the top of the lift joined them as everyone spread out, looking for trouble. Unlike the level above them, the floor of this level was made from the same material as the rest of the complex.

"Commodore, this level is wide open, empty. Orders?"

"Take the next level when ready Lieutenant." Ezra ordered.

"Yes sir."

Via the monitors Ezra watched the team load back onto the lift, first the top, then the car itself before dropping to the next level. It was a repeat of the previous level entry except this time the level wasn't empty. One of the first flares tossed into the level actually bounced back out the door which caused everyone to tense up and get ready for a fight.

It was soon evident why the flare bounced back through the door when the first person off the lift took four steps and ran into a console. As the rest of the team entered the level, they once more spread out in twos as they moved between and around what appeared to be machinery within the level.

"Anyone seeing this have any idea what we have here?" Came the call from the team leader.

"Commodore, this is Commander Sisco, it looks like they have found the complexes power source."

Commander Sisco was a Fleet Engineer who was on site to remove the flyer in the hanger.

"Lieutenant Winston, clear and secure that level then pull out. Commander Sisco, as soon as the Engineer's can light that level, I want you and anyone else you think you need in there."

"Yes Sir" Responded Winston.

"Aye, Sir." Responded Sisco.

Grave Robbing

Horner entered the Headquarters to find Ezra behind his desk going over reports that had come through during the night. Ezra looked up from his desk at Horner.

"Kevin, see if you can catch Specialist Daniels before she goes to my cabin. I have some paperwork Mister Pendergrass needs to see."

Horner chuckled. "Commodore, you haven't heard? Michele moved in with Pendergrass over a week ago."

"Moved in with him?"

"Yes Sir, it seems he has other talents besides how to handle a sharp pencil."

Ezra had to laugh at that as he shook his head.

"Then get a message to her to come in and pick up the paperwork."

"Yes Sir."

He could only imagine how that happened between who Ezra considered a meek bean counter and a Centaurian Lancer. But people often find each other as he considered Emily and himself. Both Earthlings so far from the home world, so different in their past and careers, yet they found each other.

Currently he had a dozen power plant Engineers from the Fleet down in the complex going over every millimeter of the facilities beneath the graveyard. Conventional tools were not capable of disassembling the power planet, and the Fleet Engineers spent hours designing and constructing tools to accomplish their mission.

Also there was a Fleet Forensic team moving through the graveyard tagging each body at their oddly shaped ears to later identify the place they were located in the graveyard. There was still debate between the medical personnel on how to remove them from that location in order to bag them for the trip to the surface.

One major concern was breaking the skin of an alien while digging it out. The other concern if they were in fact planted, growing in that level was the question of roots extending from their four arms and two short legs.

Ezra was just allowing the medical personnel deal with the problem as he knew the Lancers and Marines would have to do the dirty work, and he was not ready to order them in to do just that.

The Medical Forensic team finally decided they would removed the first few bodies since they had experience in such matters with humans. Once a technique was determined, they would show it to the Lancers who would continue removing the bodies as quickly as possible.

The concern over the red mold was solved by the people removing the bodies would dress in Level Four protection and go through Decon at the end of their four hour shift. This would slow down the removal but would give the Lancers a chance to get away from the gruesome task they were given.

Ezra stood before the entire Lancer Regiment and told them that any individual who finds he or she cannot deal with the task at hand, he understood and let no Lancer look down upon that person for being human. No one stepped aside as the removal progressed.

It would take nearly two months to safely remove all of the bodies as Ezra cut the work load to four days with three days off for the Lancers. In the end, they removed three thousand, six hundred, and ninety-two bodies. Even then, it was never determined if this was actually a graveyard or a garden.

The bodies were loaded onto Fleet Replenishment Freighters with their holds sealed and chilled for transit to the ice planet of Kronos for autopsy and storage. It would be decades before any final report would be issued concerning the state of the bodies.

Emily's team had done all they could do on site, and some team members went on to other locations to assist in the examination of items removed from Hildur for further testing. Others returned to New Brumsfield, to the university classrooms they taught in while writing papers on the work they had done on Hildur.

The control consoles on the upper level were carefully disassembled and transported to the Fleet Electronic Development Center on Denoyelles for reassemble and research. A massive failure occurred when a power source was hooked to it and the console caught fire, destroying it. It was determined that the console operated on a DC type power source where the source they attached to it was AC. Even at a low power, it fried the circuits and caused the fire.

The power plant was also disassembled and moved. After the console fire, it was decided not to power the system to determine how they generated power. It was disassembled piece by piece then reassembled in a computer generated model, but was never able to power the system.

The last act by the Marine Engineers, who had been on site for over two years, was to seal the cavern and the hanger with reinforced concrete. All ventilation shafts were also sealed after filling the complex with smoke to see if there were any unknown shafts still within the valley or hills.

All temporary shelters were removed from the area only leaving the more permanent structures which Ezra decided to leave in place for a time.

Closing Up Shop

The Lancers lifted first after a large party paid for by Ezra out of his pocket. Then two weeks later the Marines lifted also after a party. The only military left on the planet were the Yeomen working for both Ezra and Emily as they wrote their final reports.

Ezra could only expound on the cost in materials and manhours to search, secure, and remove the items from the tunnel complex without giving a single reason for it. He wrote commendations for the Lancer Tunnel Rats and Sappers who moved deep into the unknown to open the complex.

In the stack of commendations he wrote, he insured Captain Kevin Horner was commended for his work before and after becoming his aide. He also signed off on over a dozen commendations for the Marine Engineer's as recommended by Horner for their work in the Tunnels.

Emily wrote her reports based on the data they had gathered over the months on each item discovered and cataloged. Attached to each report was a cost analysis for each item while stating nothing was conclusive, with even some materials being undetermined at the closing of the Research Facility.

As with Ezra, she gave a complete accounting of the manhours and expense of her department showing that at great costs they had no answers concerning why the Aliens were on Hildur or their purpose for being there. She also pointed out that the material removed from the earth to construct the complex was no where to be found on the planet.

In closing, Emily pointed out that with all the hours of research, and the millions of Crowns spent doing that research, they close the project with more questions than answers, and certainly more questions about the Aliens than they had prior to the discovery of the complex.

The only known fact concerning the dead Aliens found within the main complex levels were that they all have grain in their systems. The grain was Rye, which grew wild on the planet, and it was unknown if that was the cause of death amongst the Aliens. None of the Aliens found within the graveyard had grain in their systems.

Later tests on the Aliens and the red mold determined that it was not lethal to humans, and was a result of the chemistry of the Aliens and the atmosphere they were in causing its growth. It was determined that like many molds, it could cause breathing problems in humans if inhaled in minor quantities. A warning was issued Fleet wide that respirators would be worn at all times when in contact with Alien bodies.

The intact Alien vehicle was taken to the Denoyelles Shipyards for concise examination and testing in hopes a better defense could be developed against them. The Fleet was able to utilize parts and pieces from recovered Alien ships after battles to put this craft back in flying status, but it was found to require four hands to operate it. It was later fitted with a flight computer capable of dealing with the controls and it was test flown five years after the project on Hildur was closed down.

Emily filed her final reports and resigned her commission with the Fleet. She became a housewife as she waited for Ezra to finish with his reports and submit them so he could also resign and they could start a new life together.

Mister Pendergrass made his final financial report to Ezra then caught a transport back to New Brumsfield with Michele Daniels in tow, as their relationship had blossomed along with her belly with his child.

With the complex sealed, Ezra once again took control of the surrounding area as part of his property. He looked at the forest surrounding the complex site and decided to install an additional saw mill at the location utilizing the former Research Facility buildings as storage for the lumber milled on site. There was the mess facility and other structures which could be turned into bunk houses for the men working on site to stay in during the work week, instead of having to transit back and forth daily.

When Ezra transmitted his final report and resignation, he receive a simple, two word response from the Throne; Thank You. He would also later discover a rather large bonus paid to his Exchequer account from the same private account he had received when he left the Fleet.

Before leaving Hildur, he made Isaac a minor partner in his Hildur enterprises since he had been running them since the discovery of the complex. He did the same when he took Emily to Nemea to see their home with the managers of his businesses there. This was both a bonus, and incentive to keep the businesses profitable, and expand them when possible.

Two months after arriving on Nemea, he took Emily to the one place she asked to go for a honeymoon, and that was back to Earth. They first visited with both their families as his own knew he had not died, but was still gone from their life. Once that was accomplished, he took her to the Swiss Alps and watched as she fell several times learning to ski until she mastered them. He had learned how to ski in his youth and was rusty, but the muscle memory returned quickly.

They were making love in front of a fire in the chateau he had rented when the universe was informed that Carlos Gannaway had discovered another planet, this time one with massive cities in ruin. The next morning both of them had messages wanting them to return to service, and go to this new world to oversee the exploration of the ruins.

Emily looked at Ezra and told him no, because it was time to start a family and return to Nemea to raise their children.

Ezra sent a message to the Throne asking that the Throne declare him retired from public service and not to bother him again.

There was no response to the message, but when they transited from Earth for Nemea, the Fleet signaled to the Cherry Blossom: "Fair winds and following seas, Commodore."

Ezra was finally free of guilt and the burden of responsibility to the Federation. Emily was his only life from that day on.

About The Author

Leon Michaels is the author of several novels and short stories that reflect his twenty-three years of military service.   Michaels enlisted in the Marine Corps in 1970 and has memberships in the Veterans of Foreign Wars, the American Legion, the Disabled American Veterans organizations, NRA, and Rotary International.   In 1971, he married his high school sweetheart, raised three daughters and has three grandsons. He calls Creek County, Oklahoma home.